Secret Path

Gord Downie + Jeff Lemire

Published by Simon & Schuster

New York London Toronto Sydney New Delhi

Simon & Schuster Canada
A Division of Simon & Schuster, Inc.
166 King Street East, Suite 300
Toronto, Ontario M5A 1J3

This Simon & Schuster Canada edition October 2016

SIMON & SCHUSTER CANADA and colophon are registered trademarks
of Simon & Schuster, Inc.

For information about special discounts for bulk purchases,
please contact Simon & Schuster Special Sales at 1-800-268-3216
or CustomerService@simonandschuster.ca.

Library and Archives Canada Cataloguing in Publication
Downie, Gordon, 1964-, author
Secret path / Gord Downie & Jeff Lemire.
Issued in print and electronic formats.
ISBN 978-1-5011-5594-9 (paperback).--ISBN 978-1-5011-5596-3 (ebook)
1. Songs, English--Canada--Texts. 2. Popular music--Canada--
Texts. I. Lemire, Jeff, illustrator II. Title.
ML54.6.D752 2016 782.42026'8 C2016-902785-6
C2016-902786-4

Manufactured in Canada

3 5 7 9 10 8 6 4 2

ISBN 978-1-5011-5594-9
ISBN 978-1-5011-5596-3 (ebook)

Secret Path

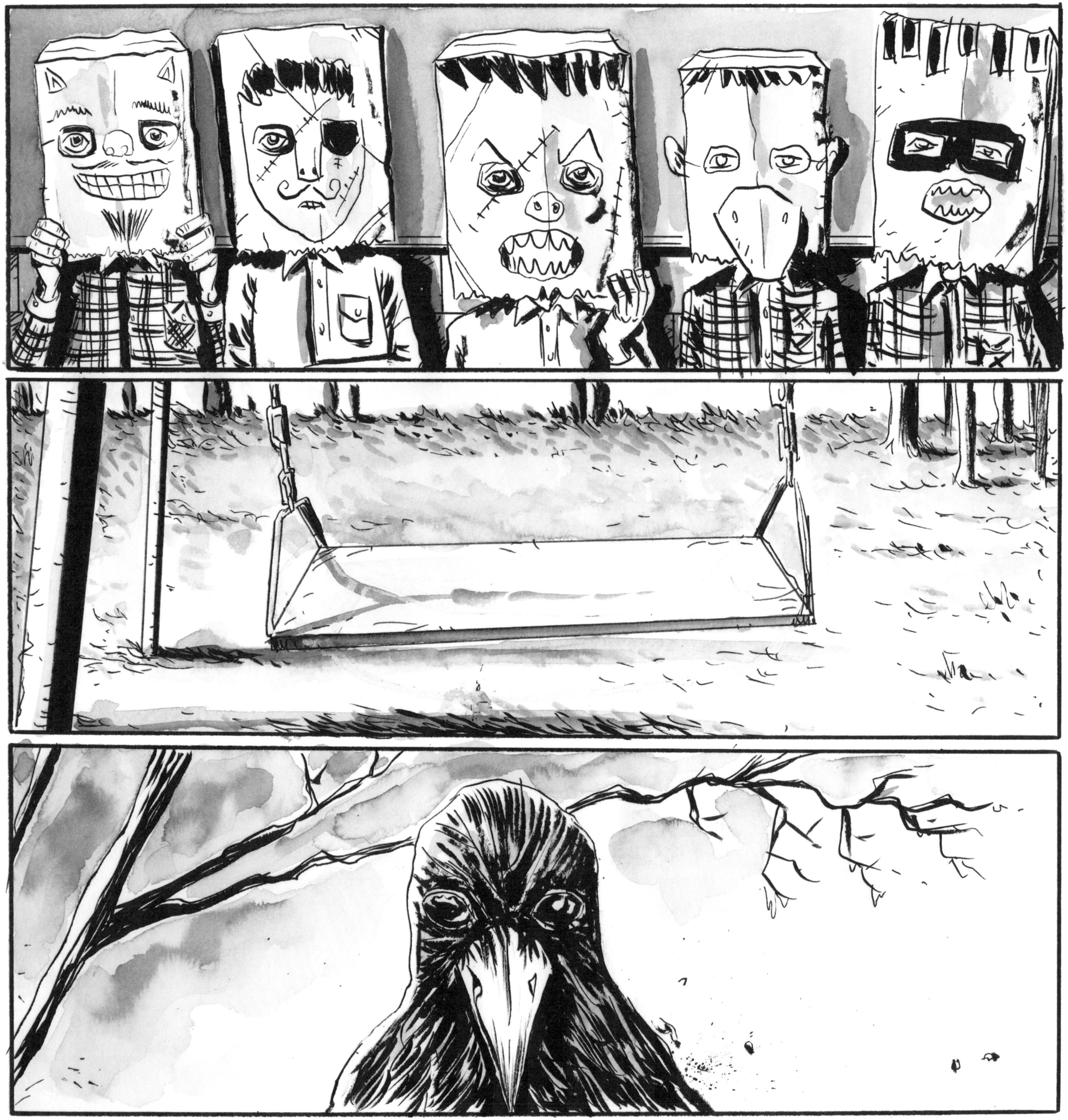

THE STRANGER

I am the Stranger
You can't see me
I am the Stranger
Do you know what I mean?

I navigate the mud
I walk above the path
Jumping to the right
And I jump to the left

On the Secret Path
The one that nobody knows
And I'm moving fast
On the path that nobody knows

And what I'm feeling
Is anyone's guess
What is in my head
And what's in my chest

I'm not gonna stop
I'm just catching my breath
They're not gonna stop
Please, just let me catch my breath

I am the Stranger
You can't see me
I am the Stranger
Do you know what I mean?

That is not my dad
My dad is not a wild man
He doesn't even drink
My daddy's not a wild man

On a Secret Path
The one that nobody knows
And I'm moving fast
On the path nobody knows

I am the Stranger
I am the Stranger
I am the Stranger

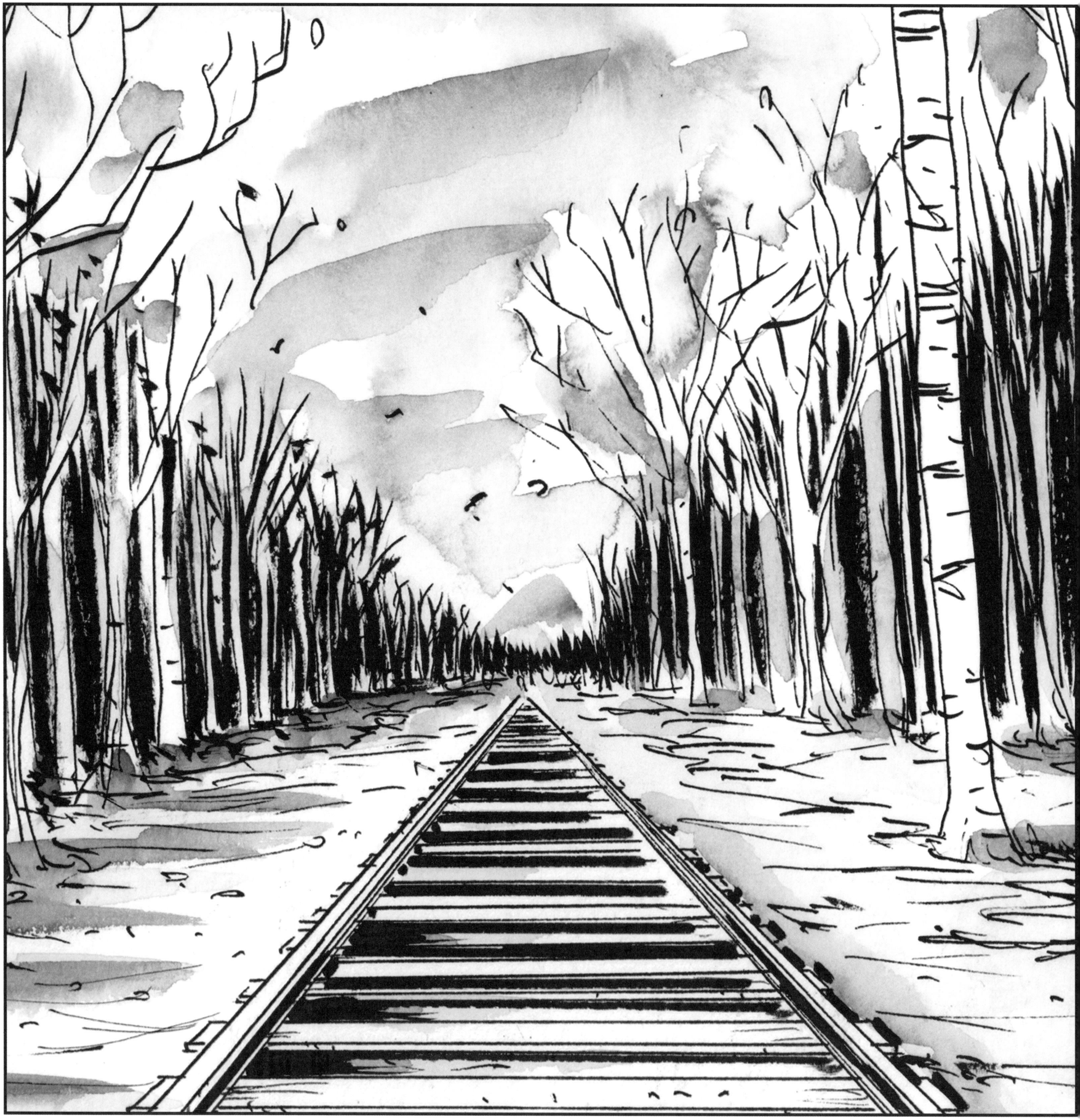

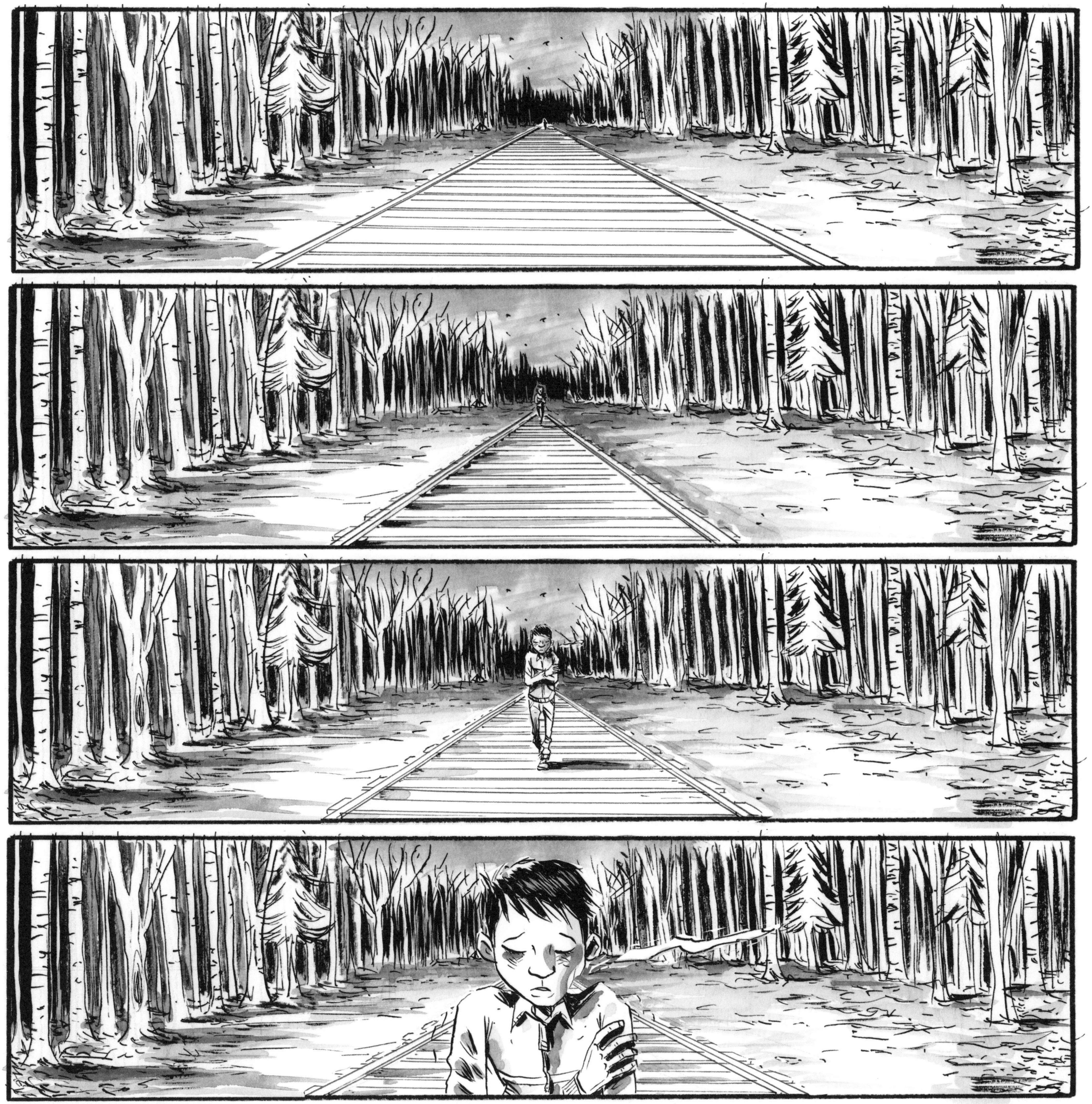

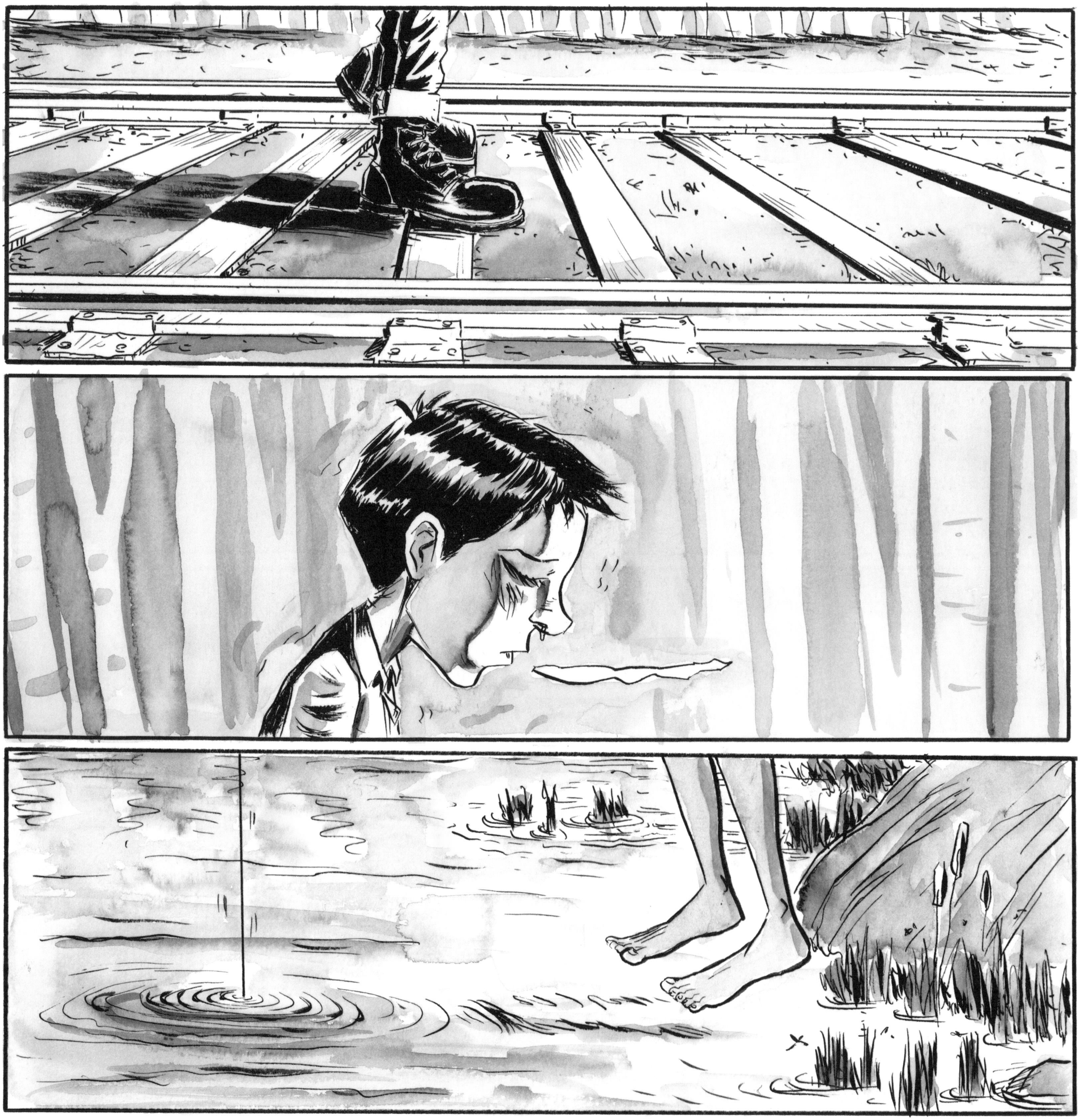

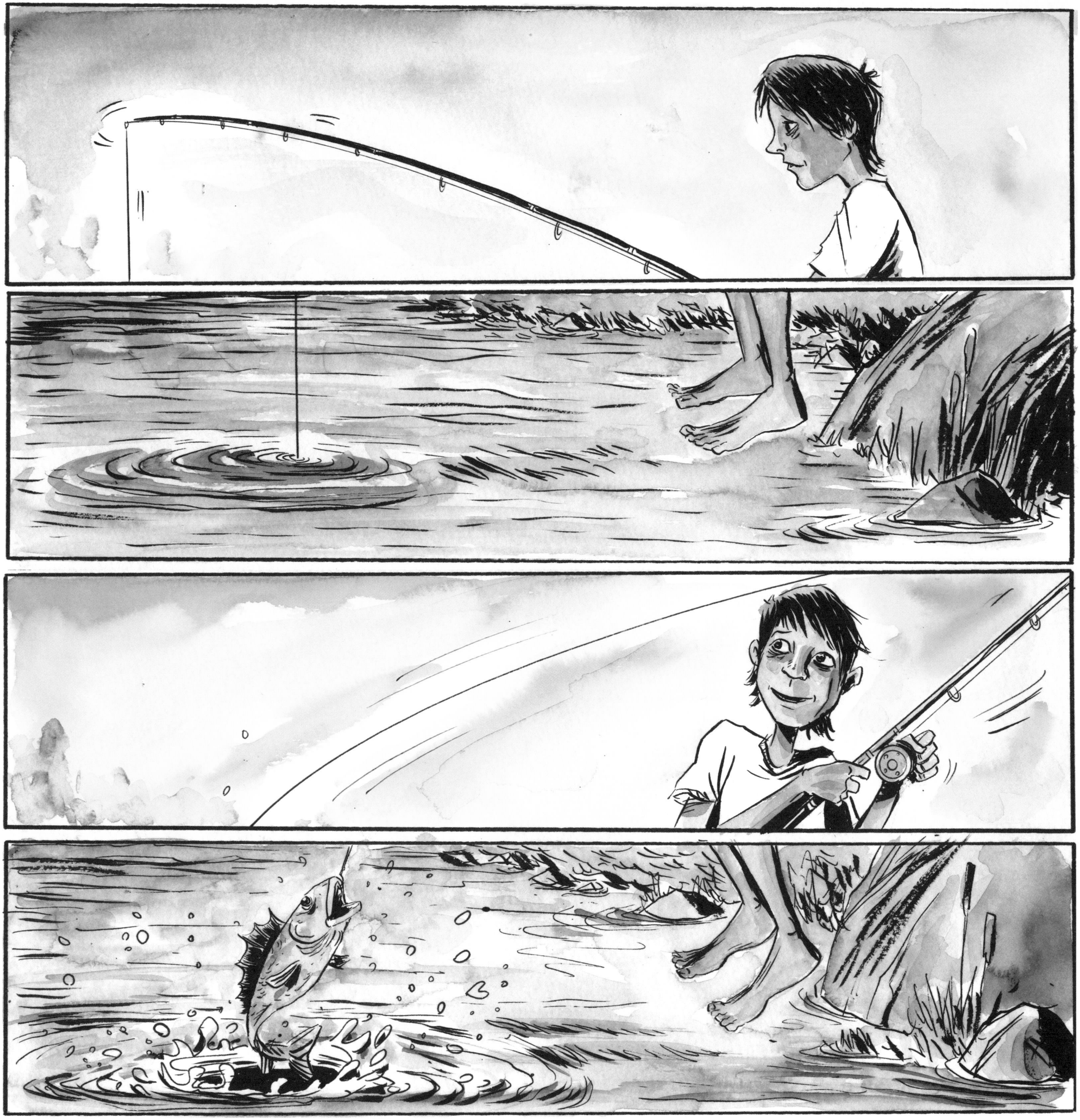

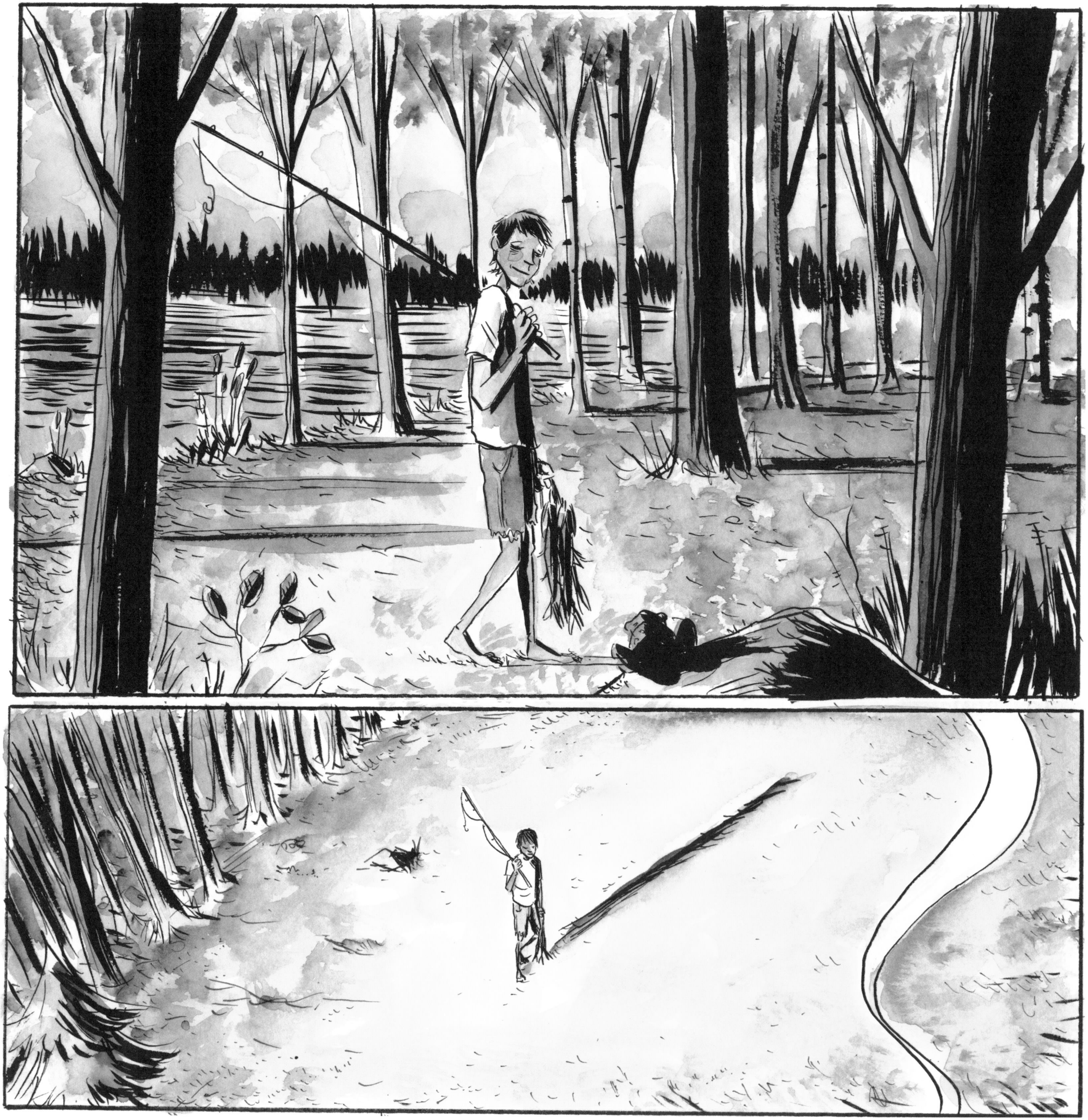

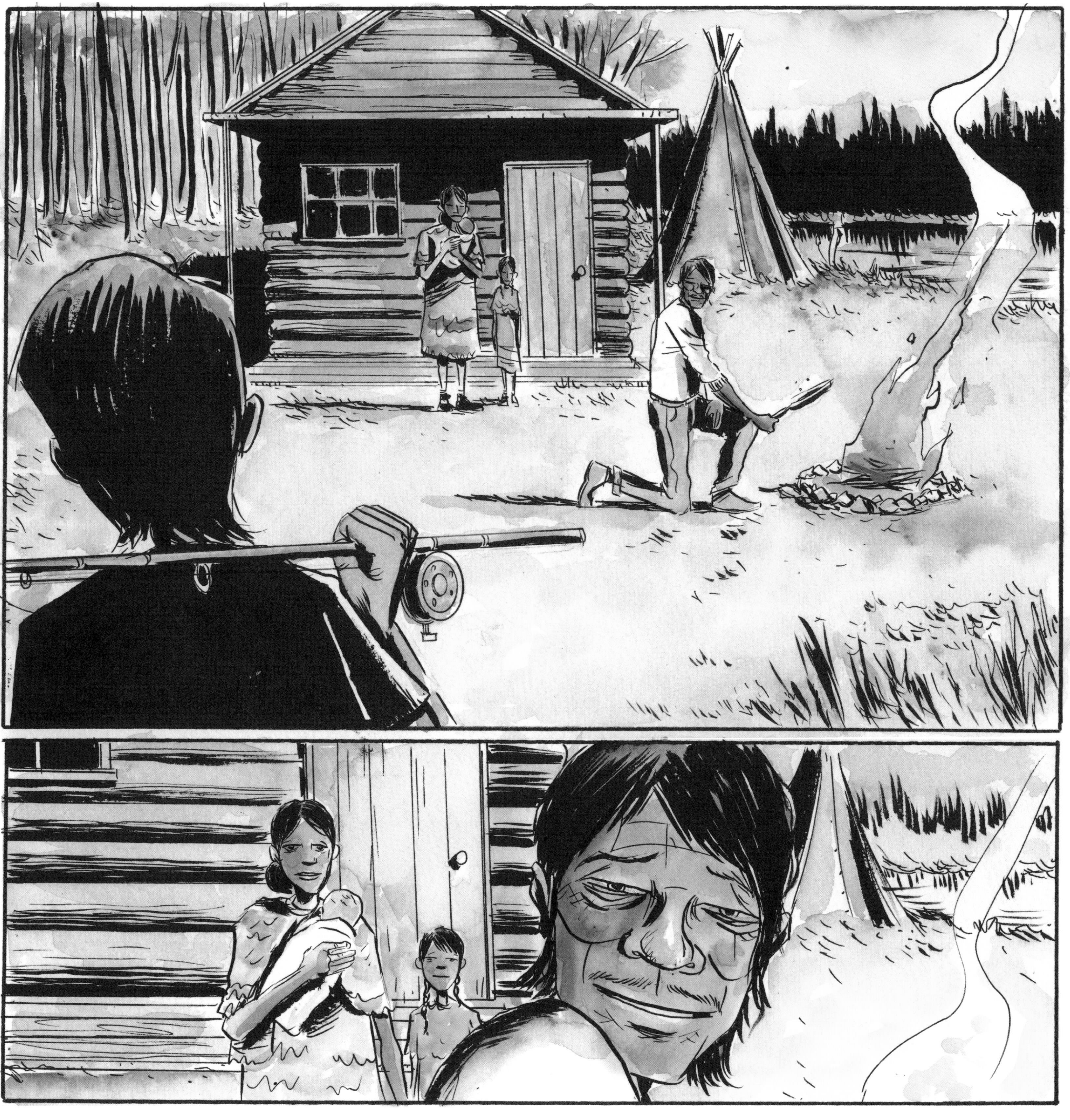

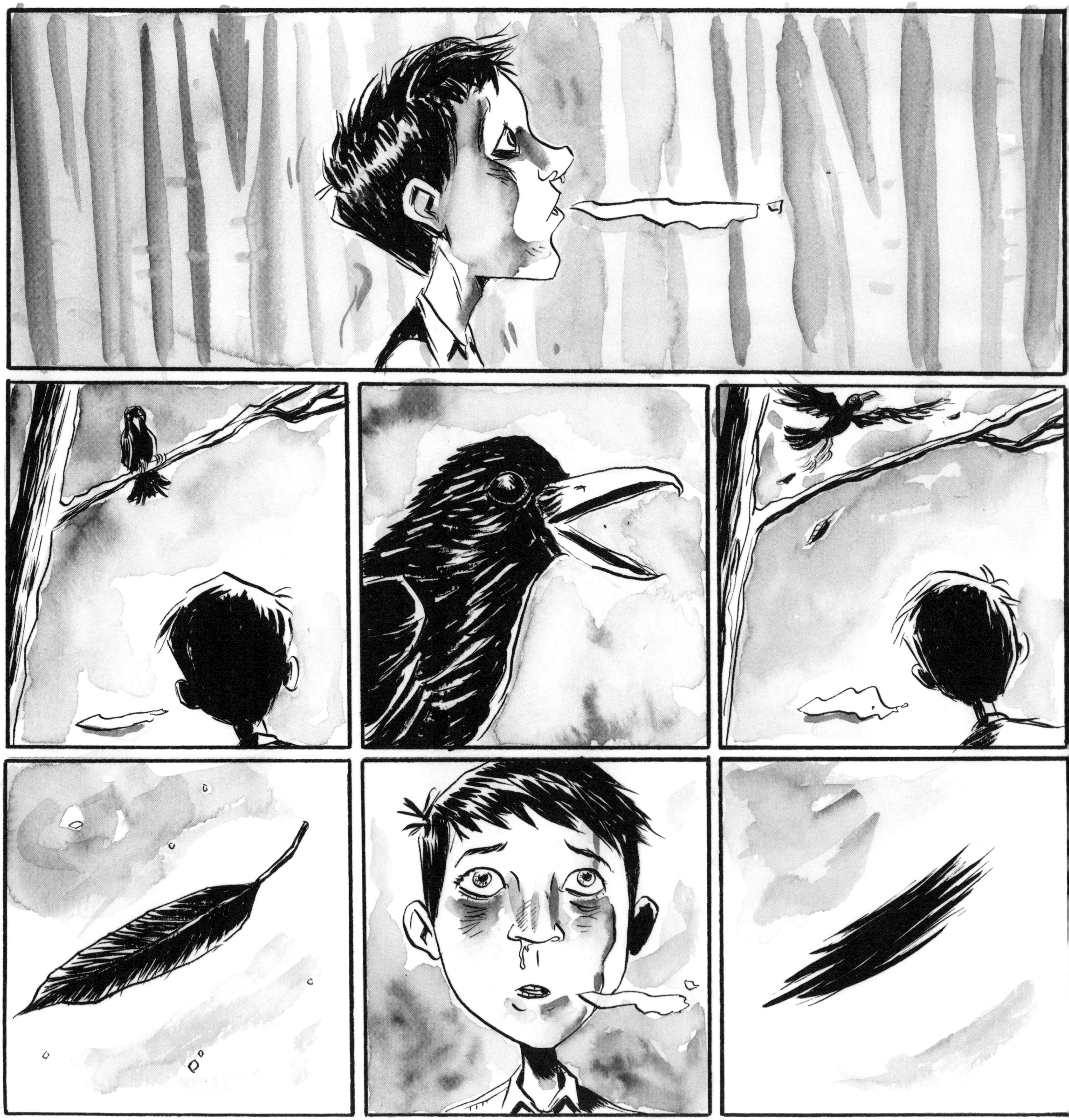

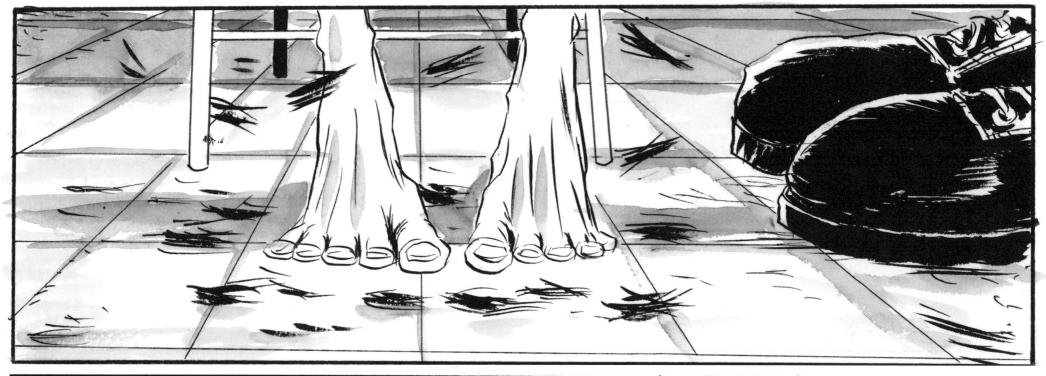

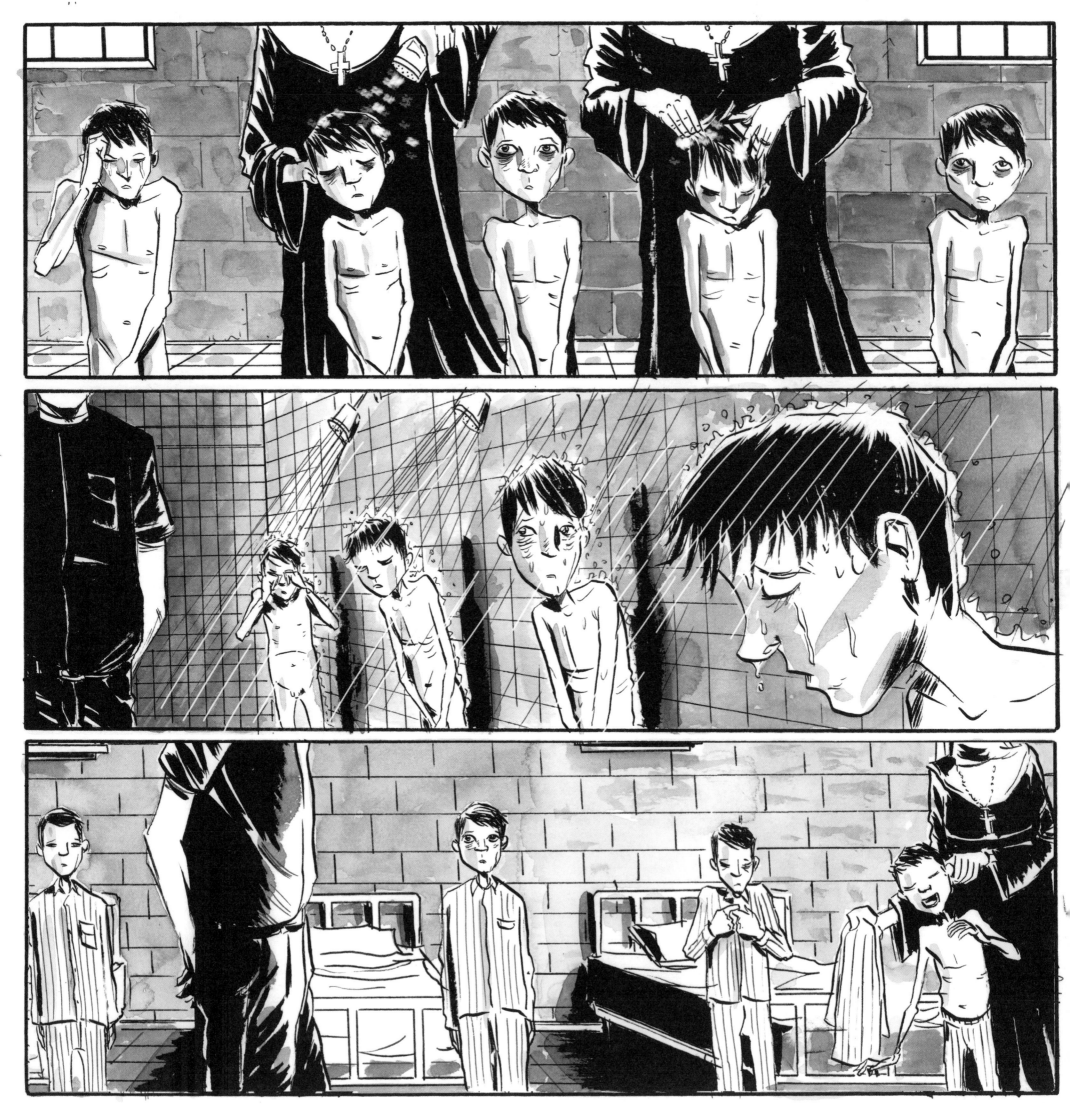

                    SWING SET

                    We were at
                    The swing set
                  "Now?" I asked
                  "Not yet," you said

        Turning round and round in my seat
          Chains twining over my head
          When the tension is complete
          And there is no way out of it

                    "Now?"
                    "Not yet."
                    "Now?"
                    "Not yet."

            Over the rise on the lawn
            Someone dragging someone
          The kid looking me in the eye
          Teacher not looking at anyone

                    "Now?"
                    "Not yet."
                    "Now?!"
                    "Now. Yes."

          I looked behind me only once
          Didn't see nobody chasing us
      Just my swing dancing in the sun
          Dancing wildly where it was

                    Now?
                    Now. Yes.
                    Now?
                    Now. Yes.

                    Now. Yes.
                    Now. Yes.
                    Now. Yes.
                    Now. Yes.

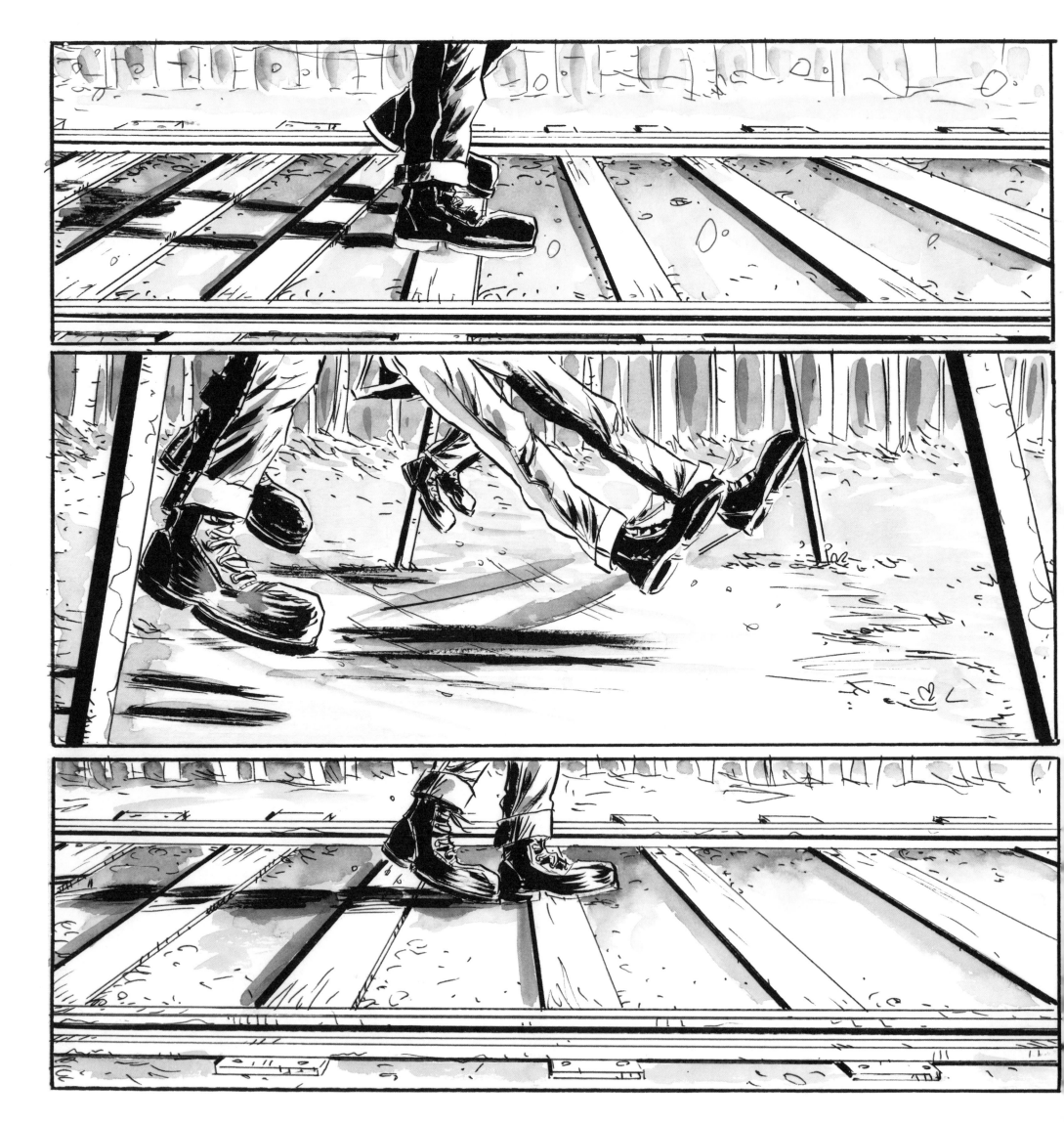

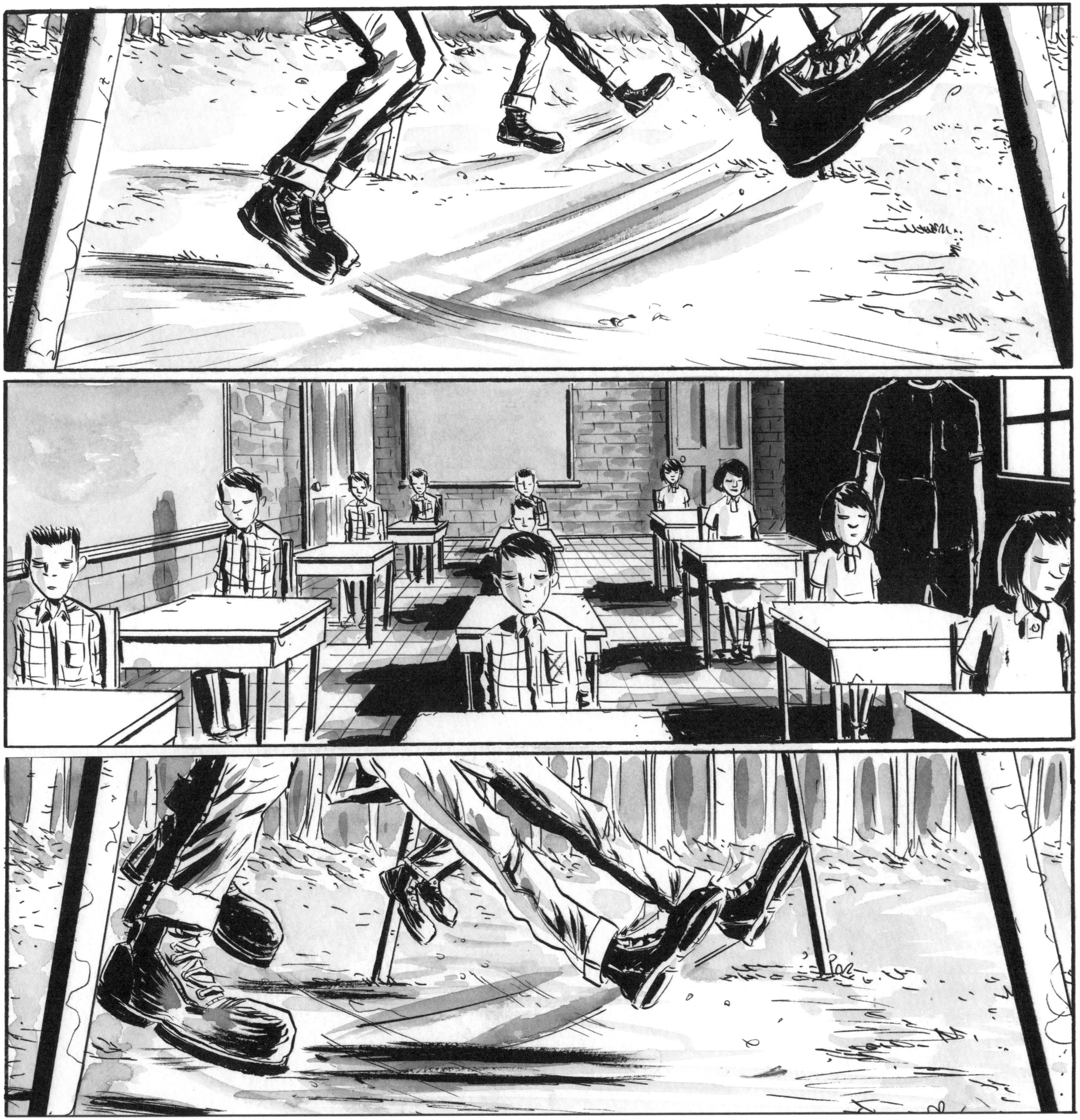

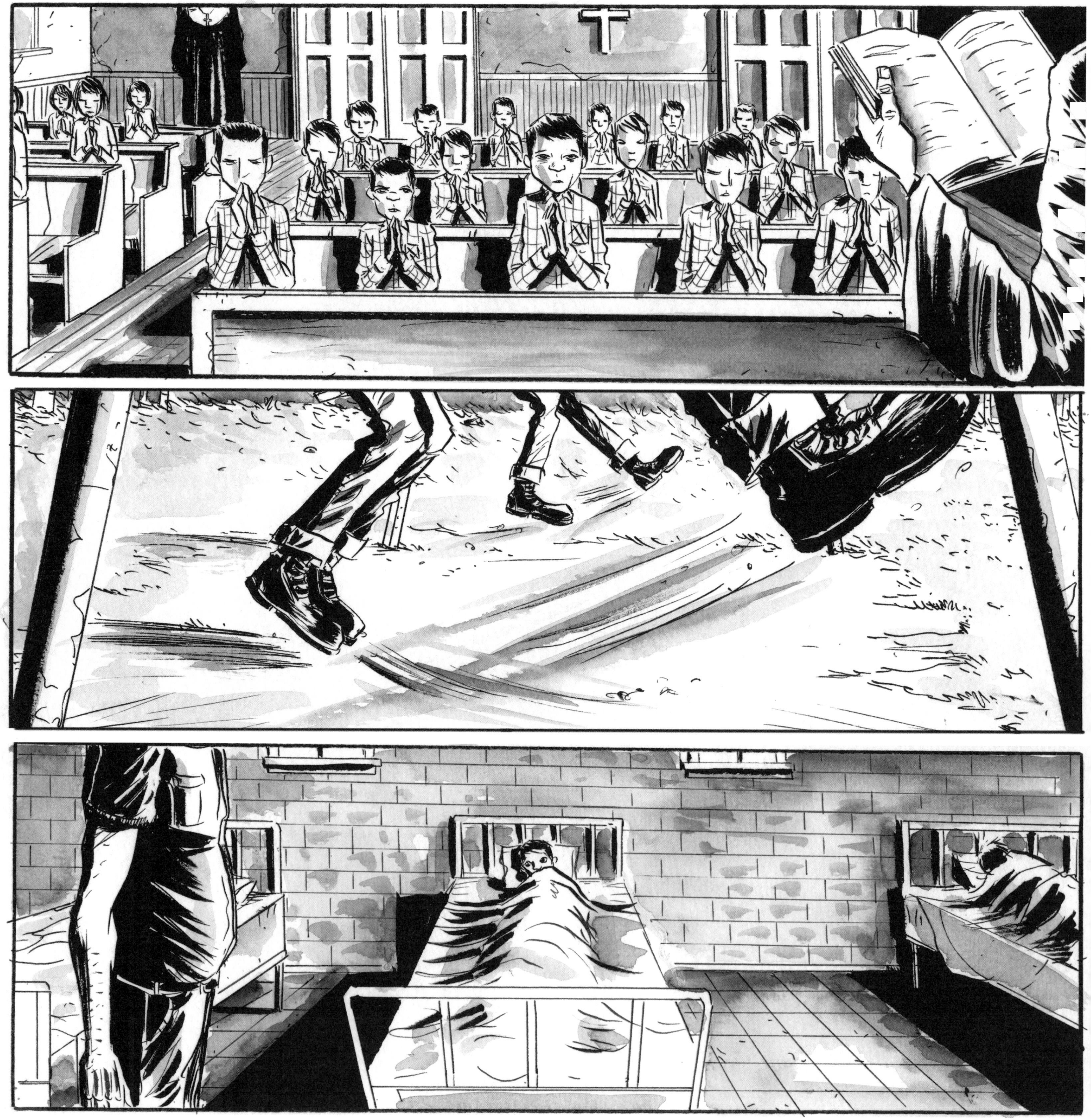

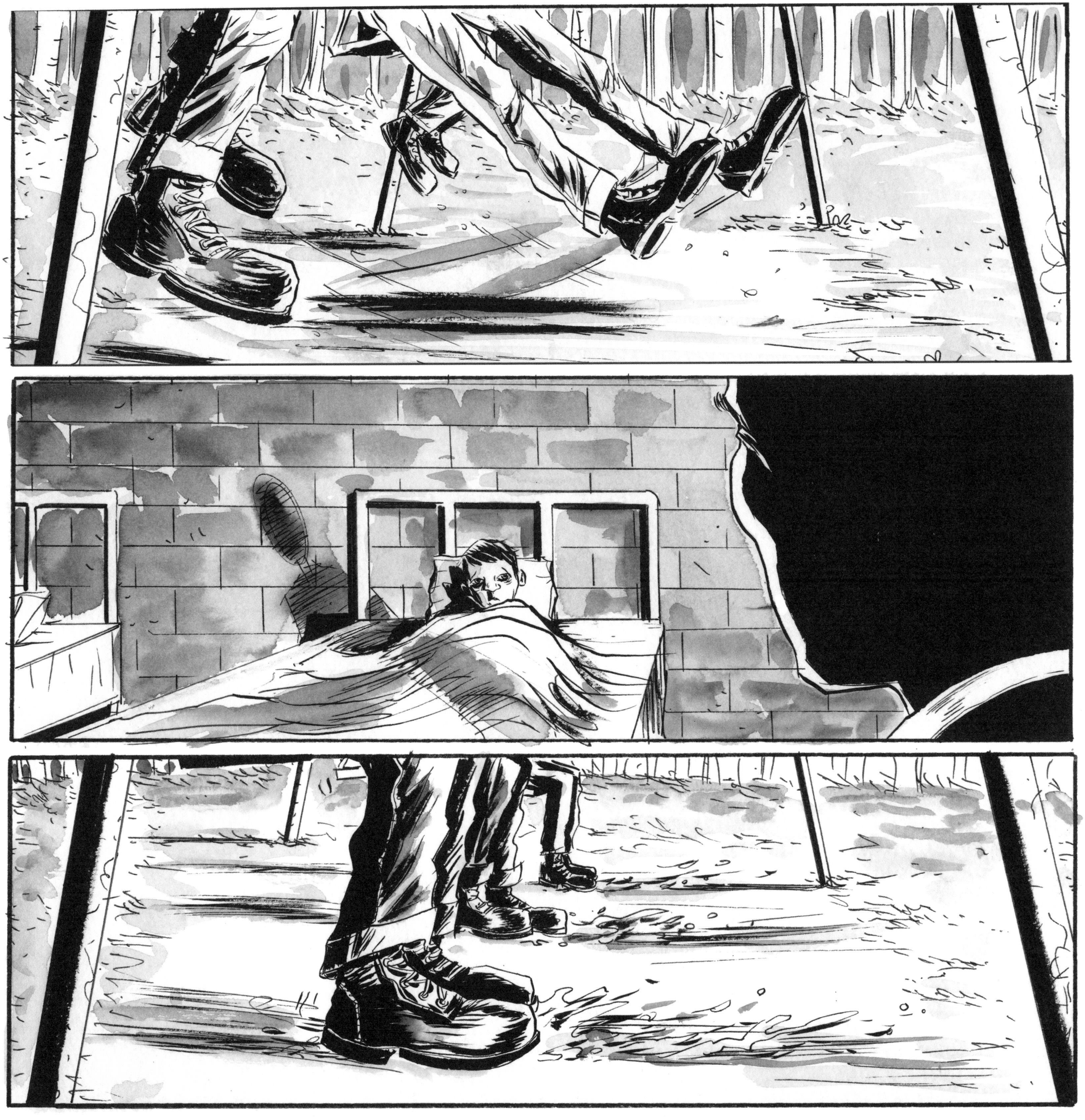

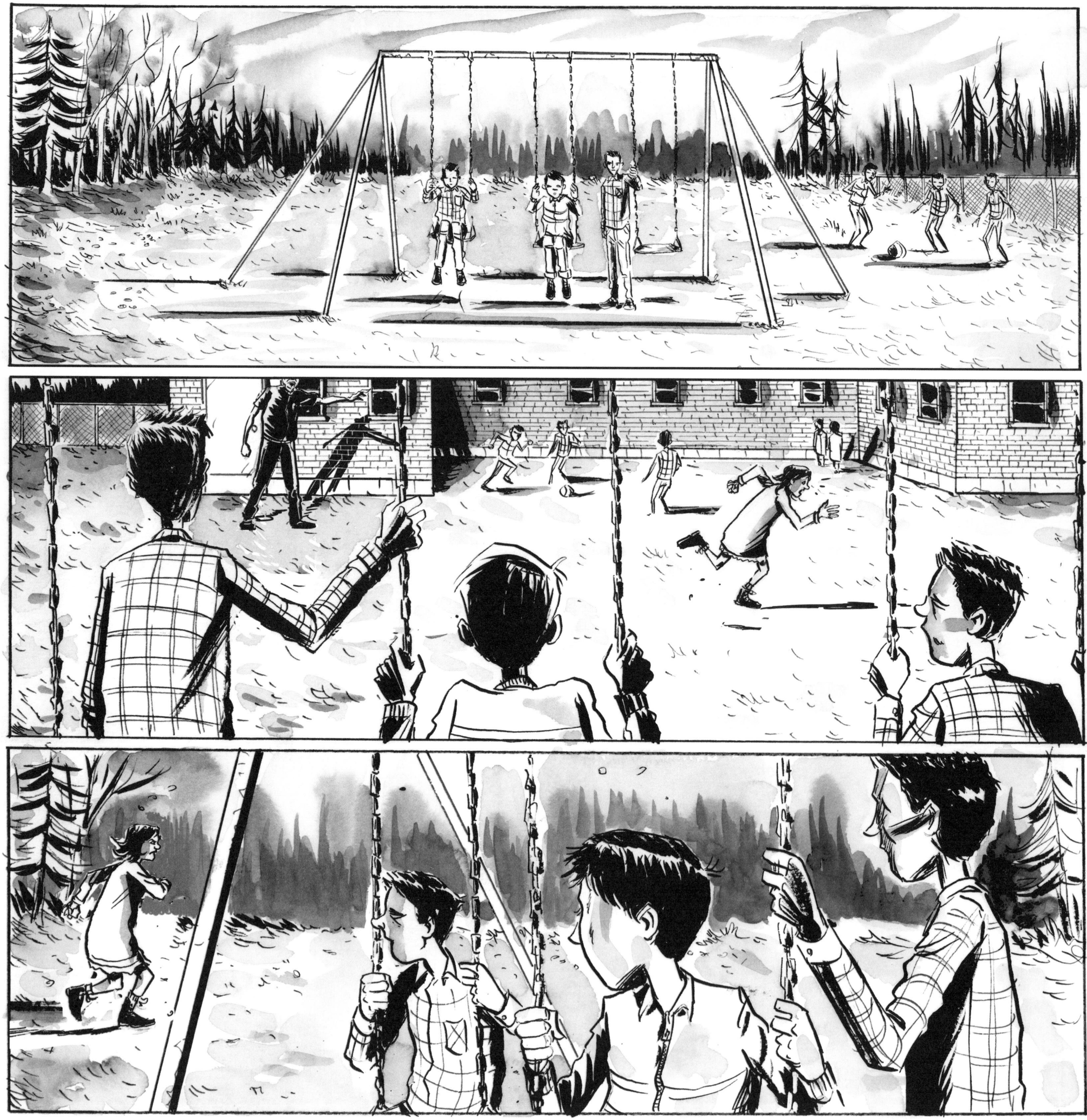

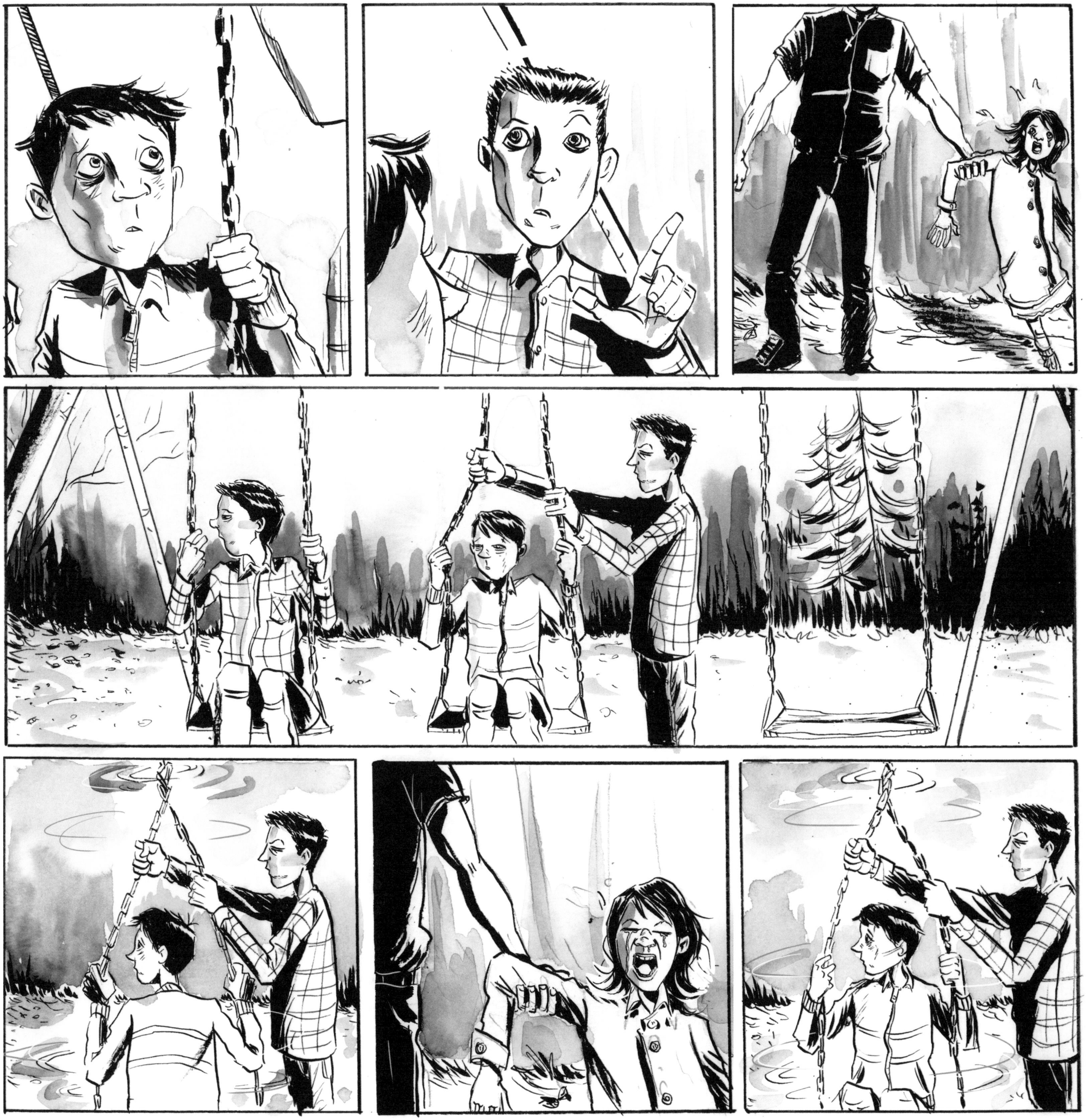

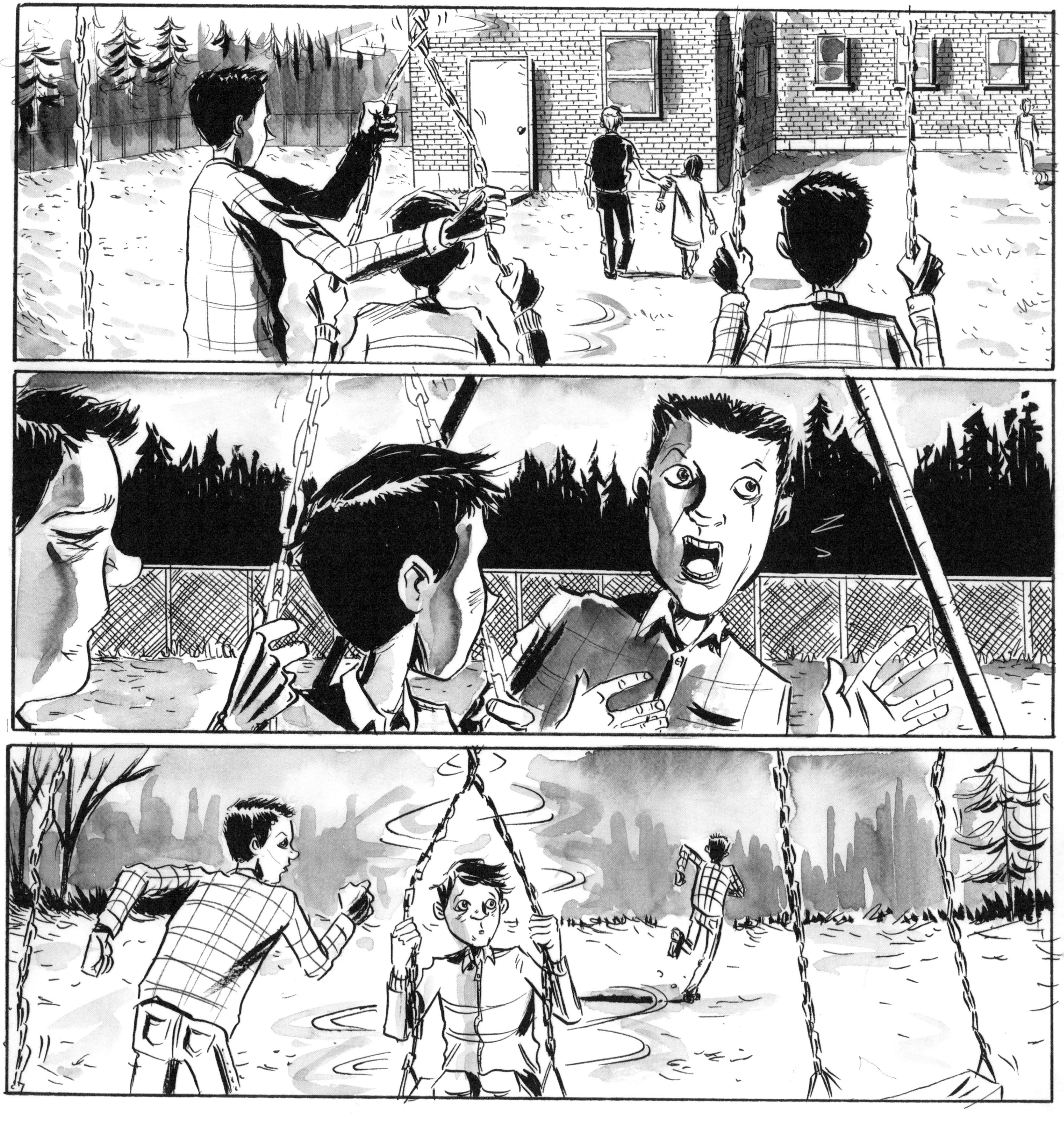

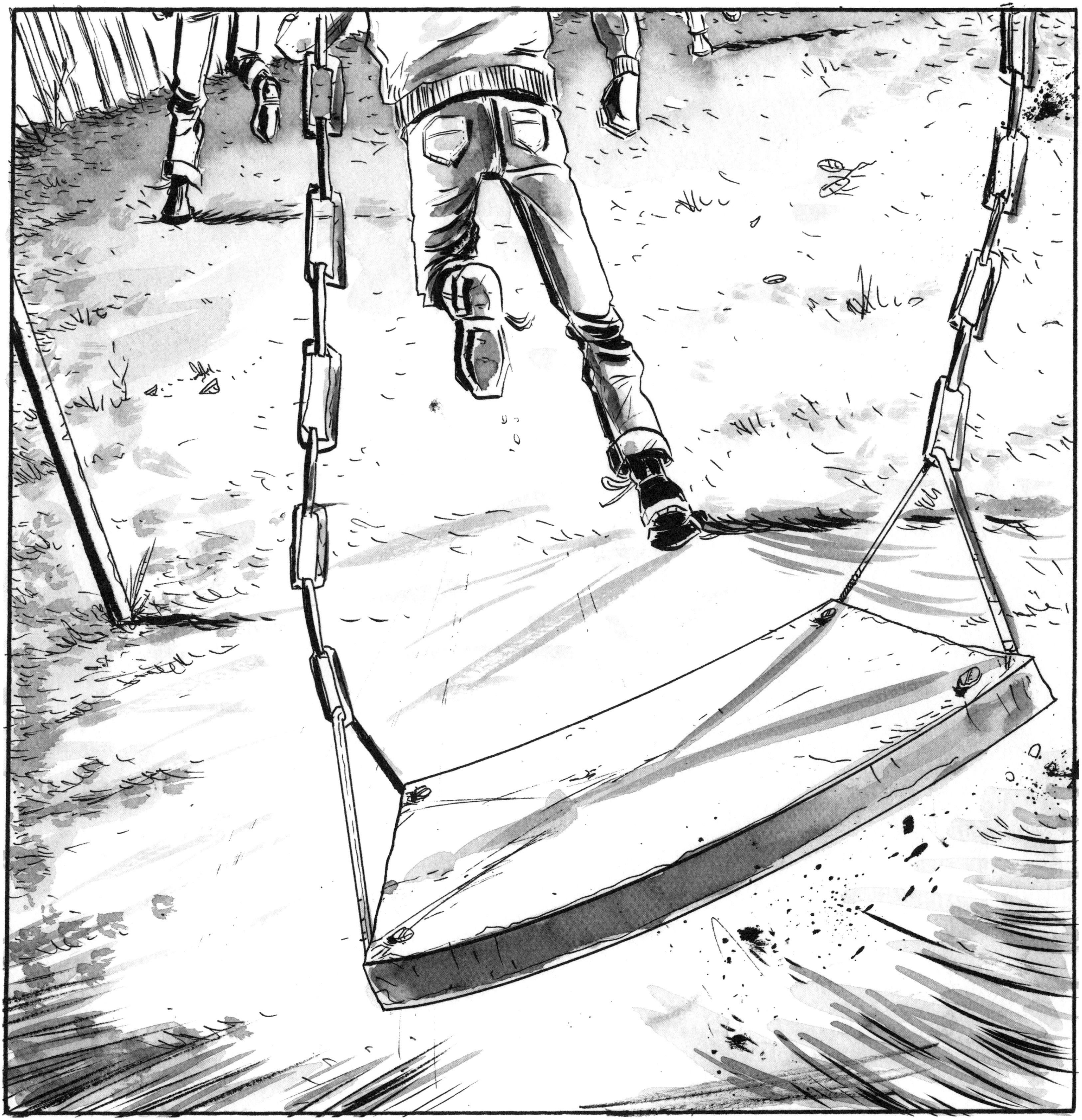

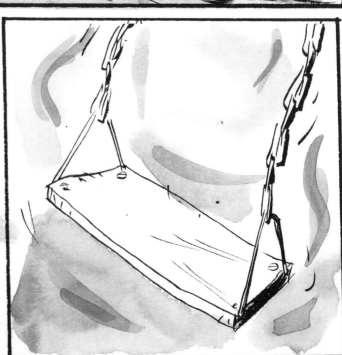

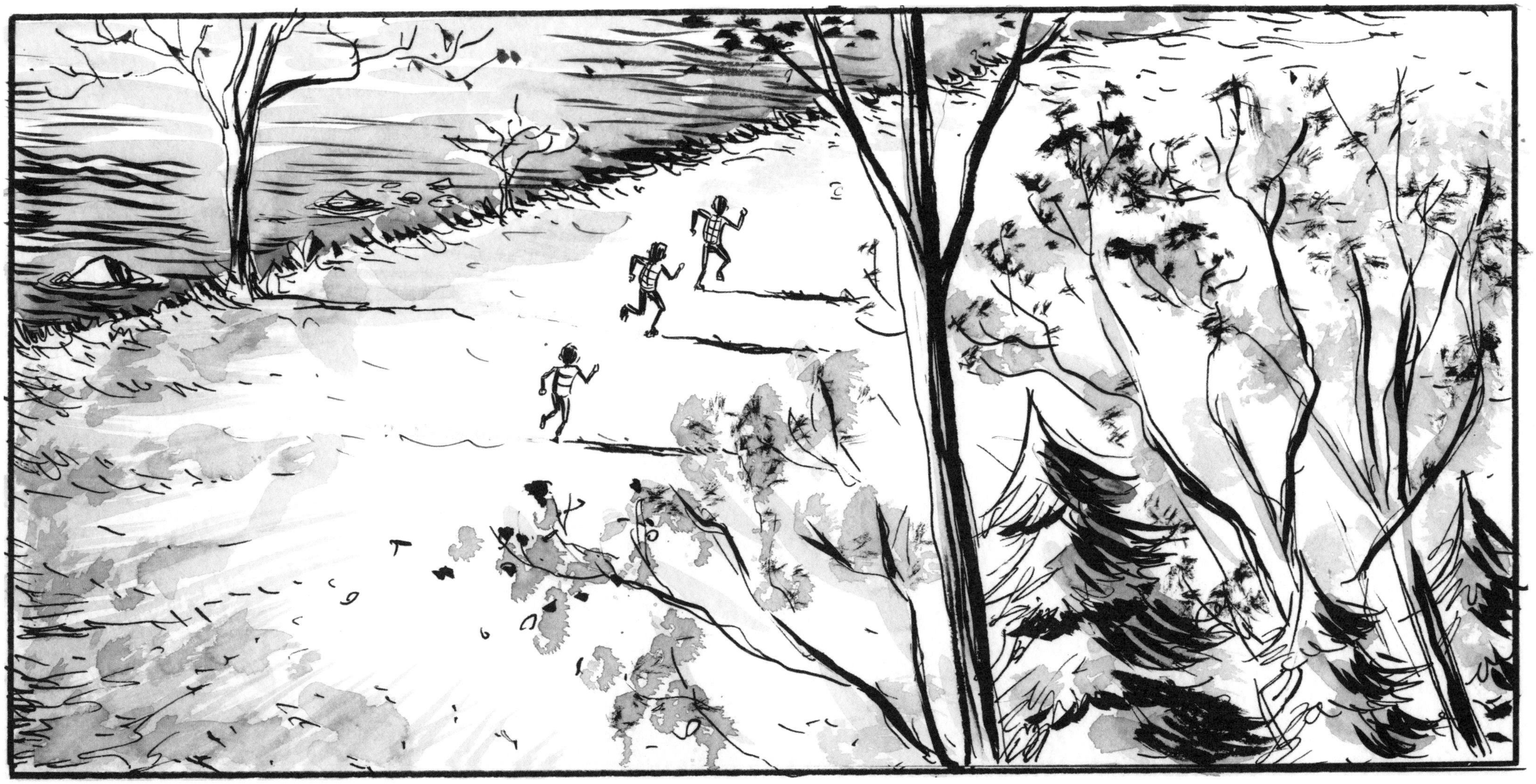
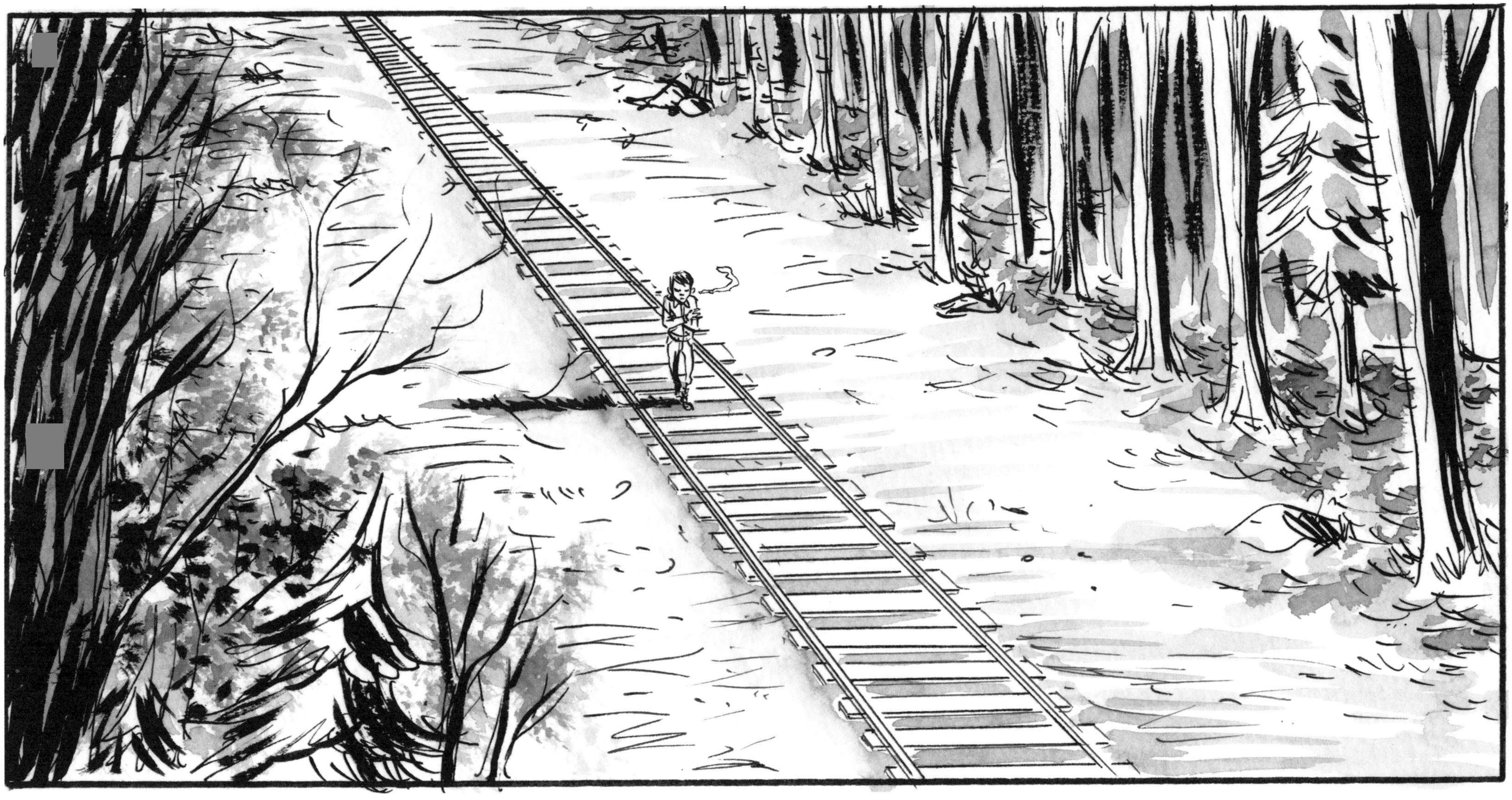

SEVEN MATCHES

She gave me matches
Seven wooden matches
She put them into a small slim glass jar
With a screwtop lid

I fingered that jar
I put it in my pocket
She said, "Can't go into the woods without them."
I smiled at her and left

And I kept them dry
And as long as there were six
I'd be fine
As long as there were five

Matches in that jar
Mile after mile
On the chick-chick chick-chick sound of the matches
On the memory of her smile

I kept them dry
And as long as there were five
I'd be fine
As long as there were four

Matches in a jar
With a screwtop lid
I know she did not mean to hurt my feelings
But that's what she did

And I kept them dry
And as long as there were three
I'd be fine
As long as there were two

Matches in that jar.

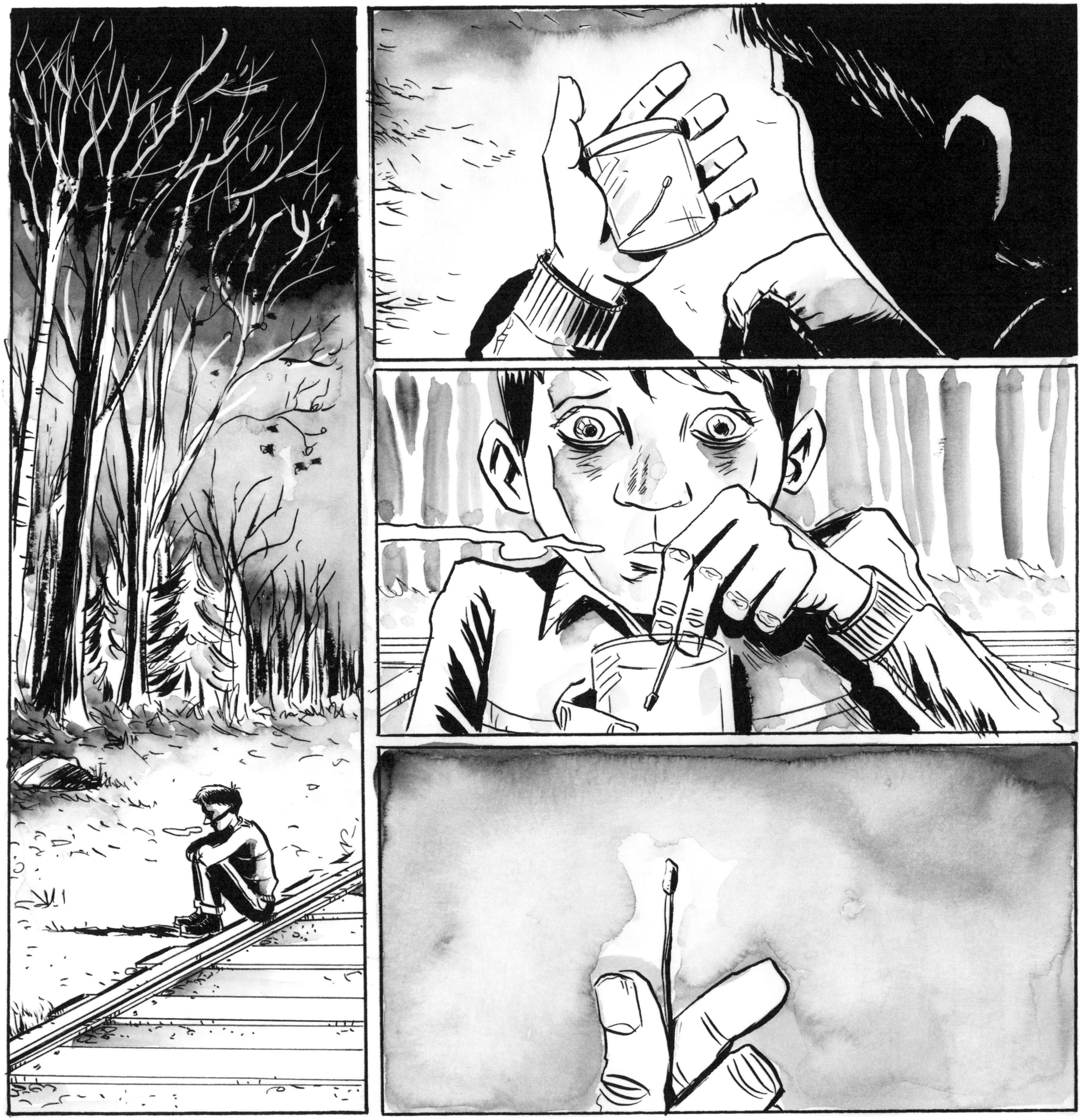

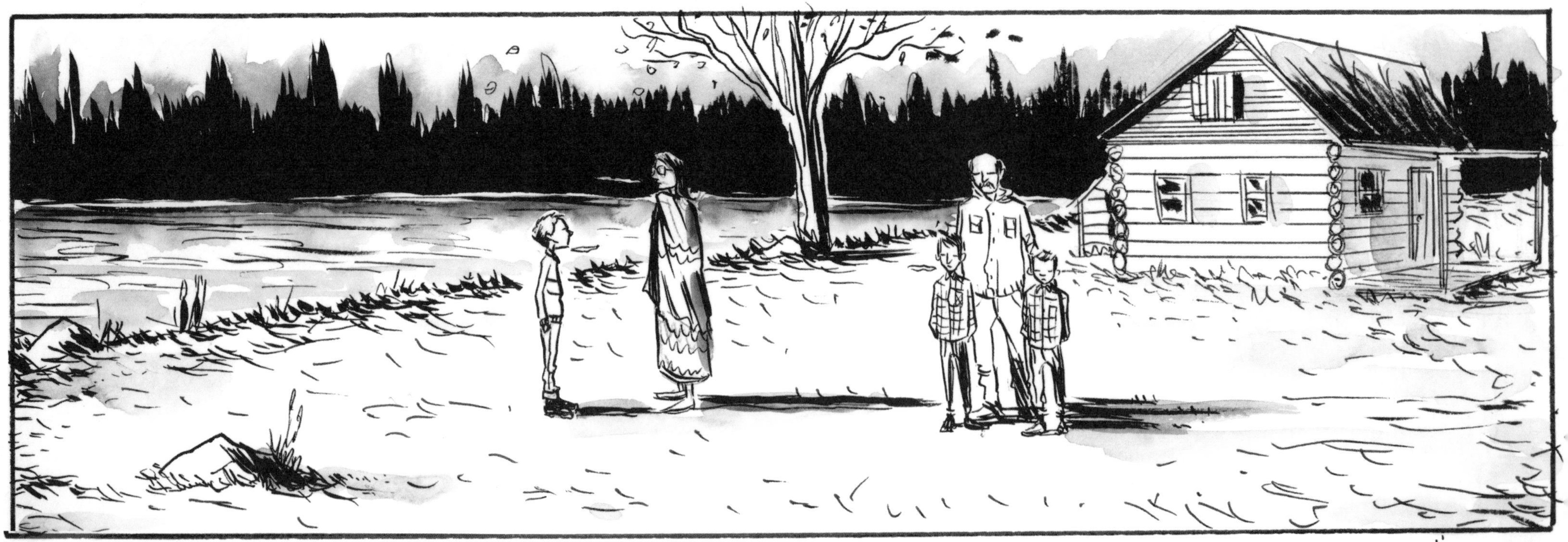

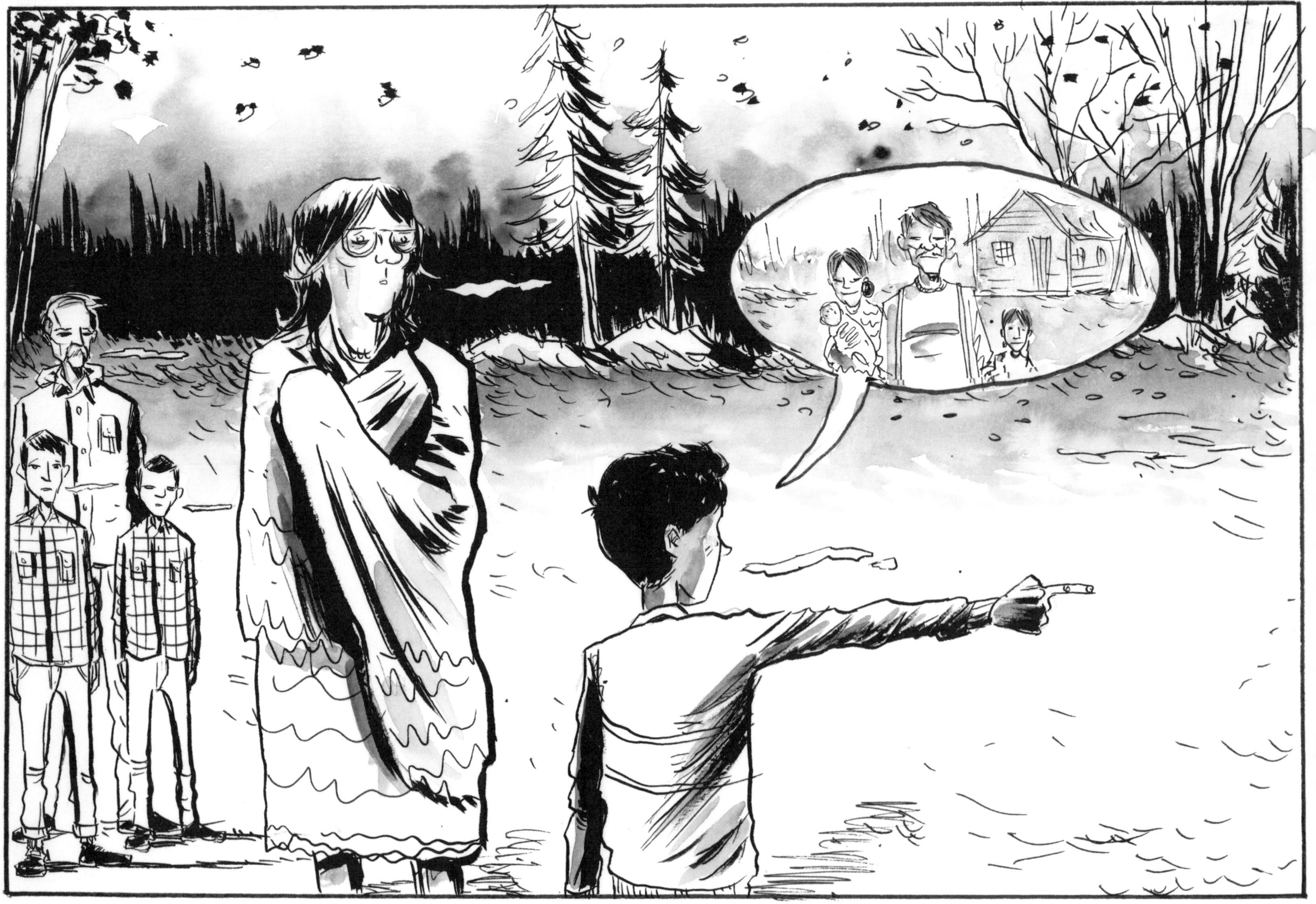

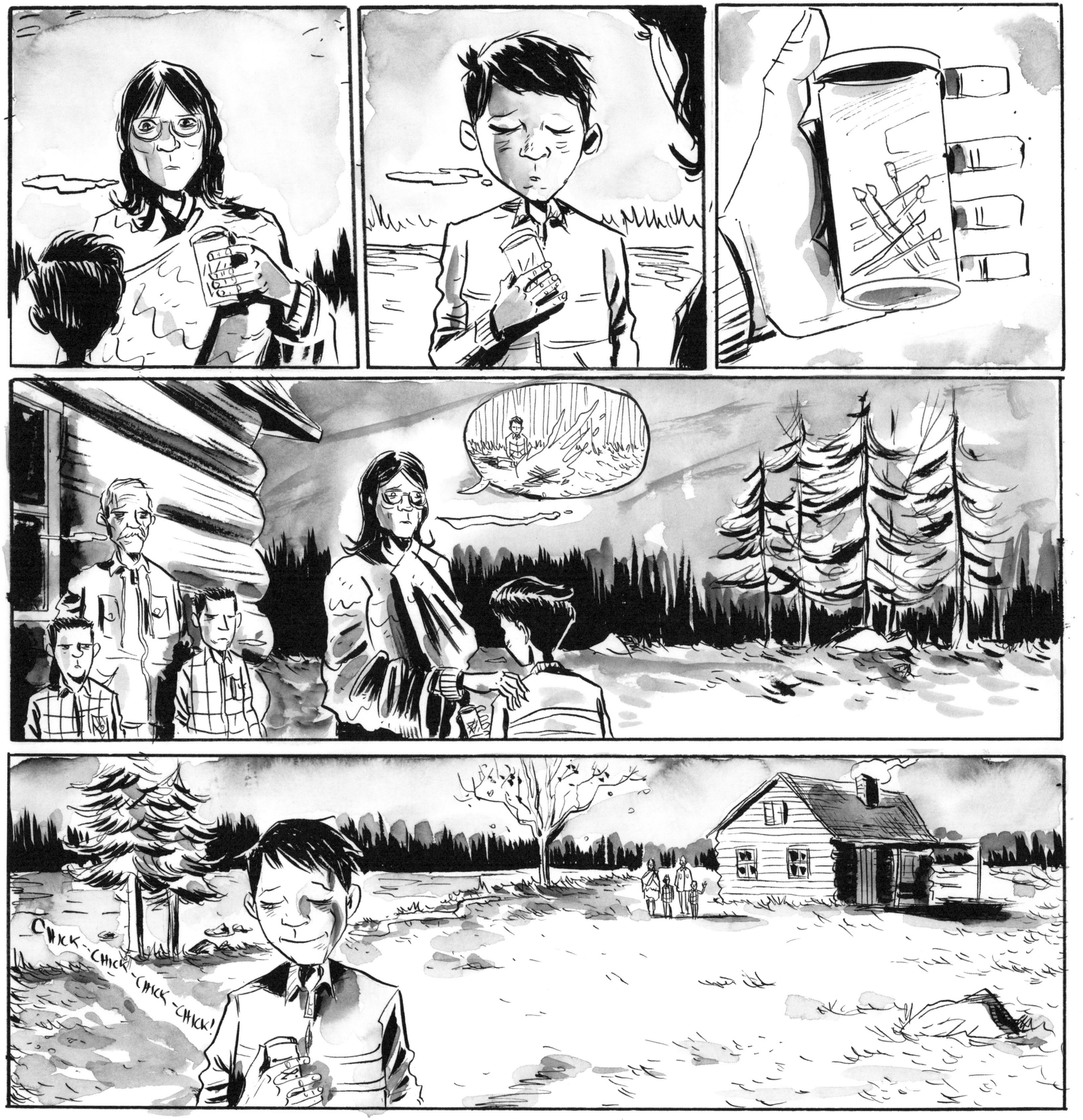
CHICK-CHICK-CHICK-CHICK!

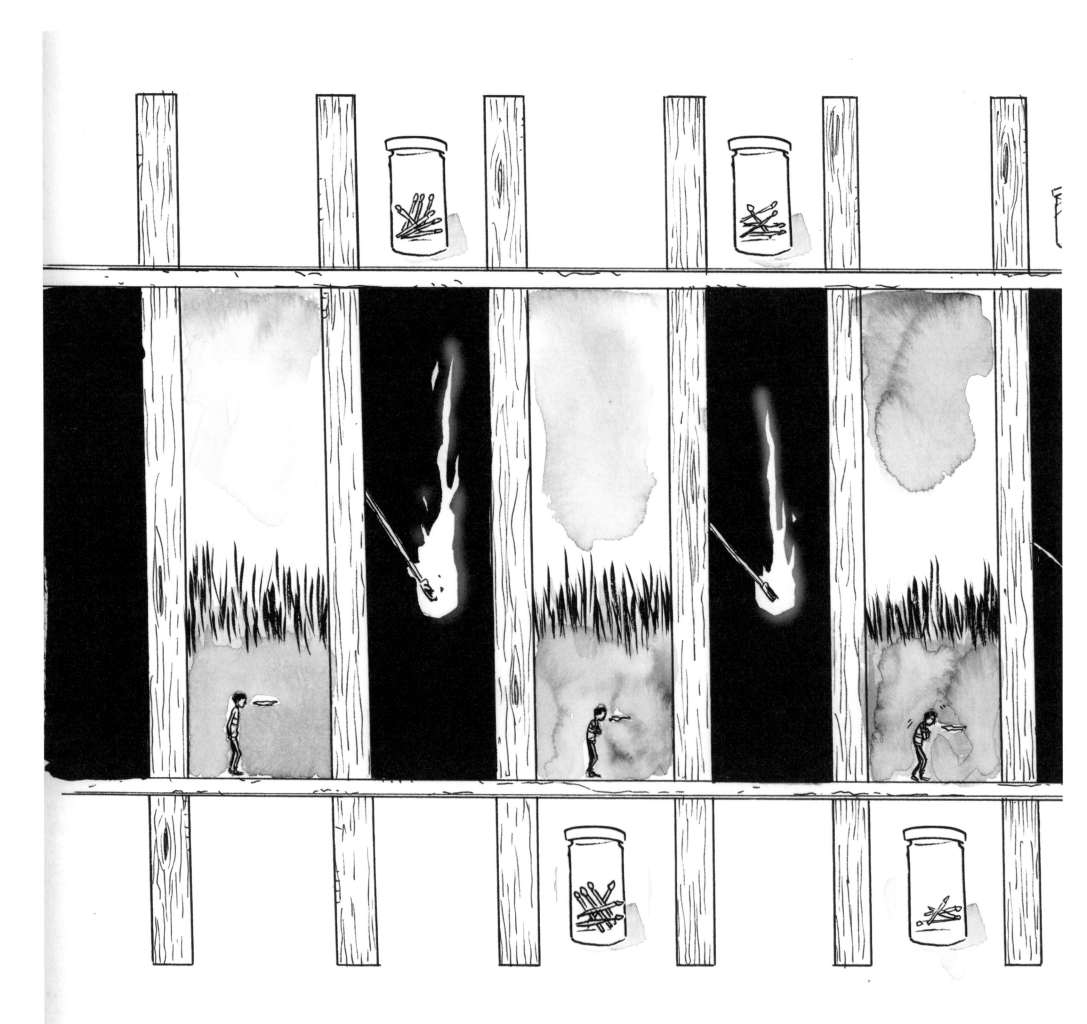

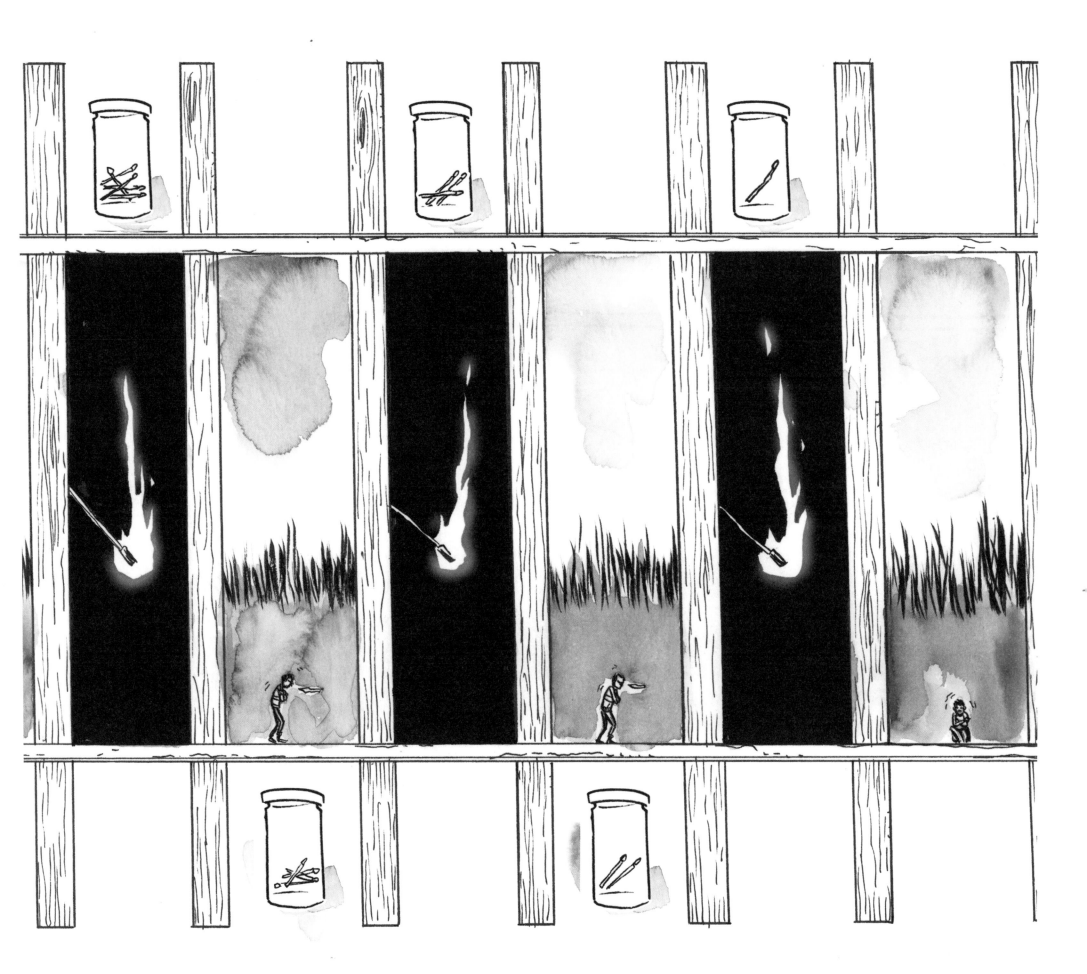

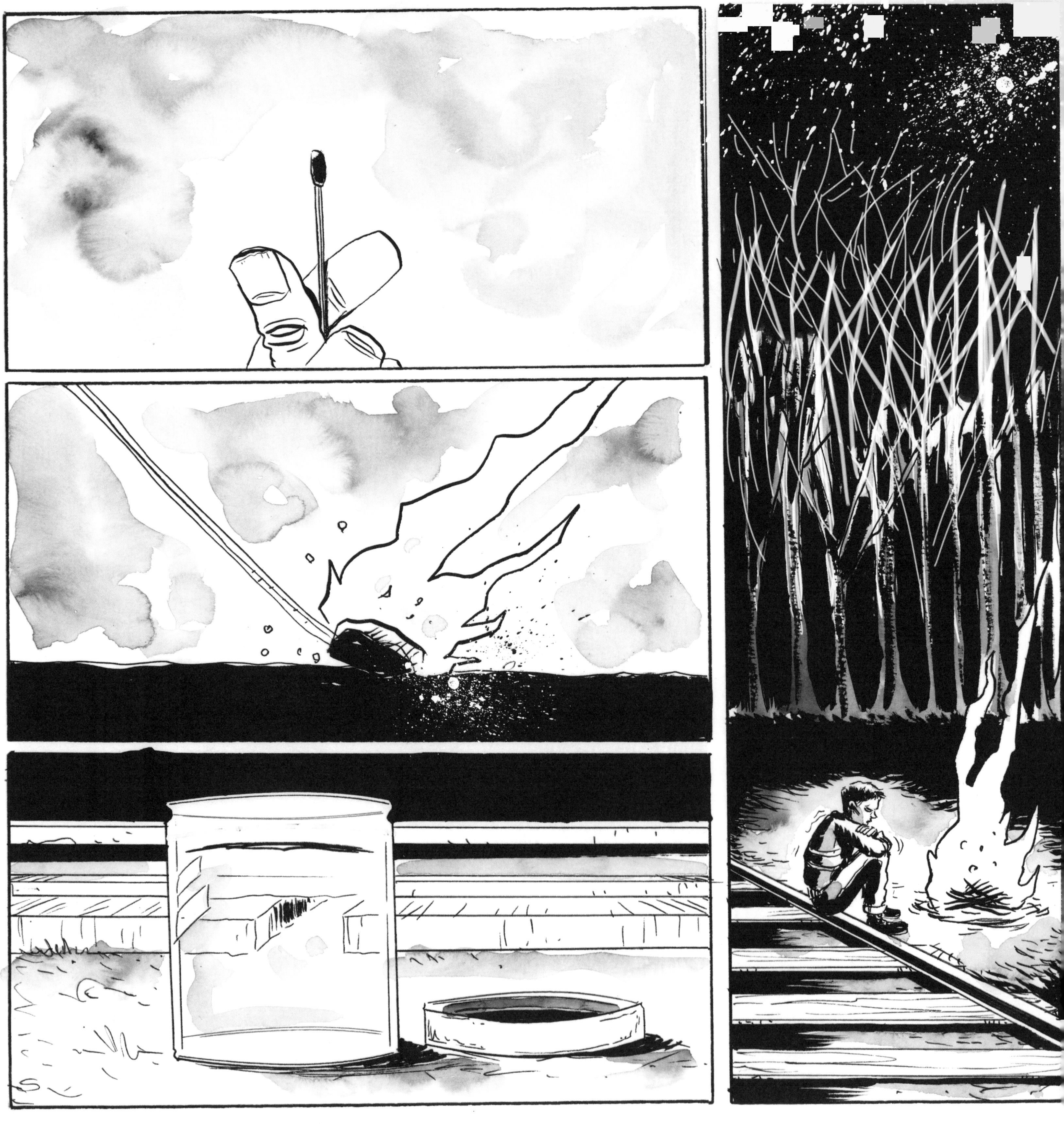

I WILL NOT BE STRUCK

In this earthlike world
In this earthlike world
Before they arrived

Under this sunlike star
Under the sunlike star
They civilized

Run along the river
On the Secret Path
I will not be struck
I'm not going back

And I see my father's face
Warming his feet by the stove
We used to have each other
Now we only have ourselves

Then I put my ear
Then I put my ear
Right against the rail

So what I couldn't hear
What I couldn't hear
I would feel

Run along the river
Along the Secret Path
I will not be struck
I'm not going back

I am staring into space
Forever or else
Enter the wilderness
And we only have ourselves

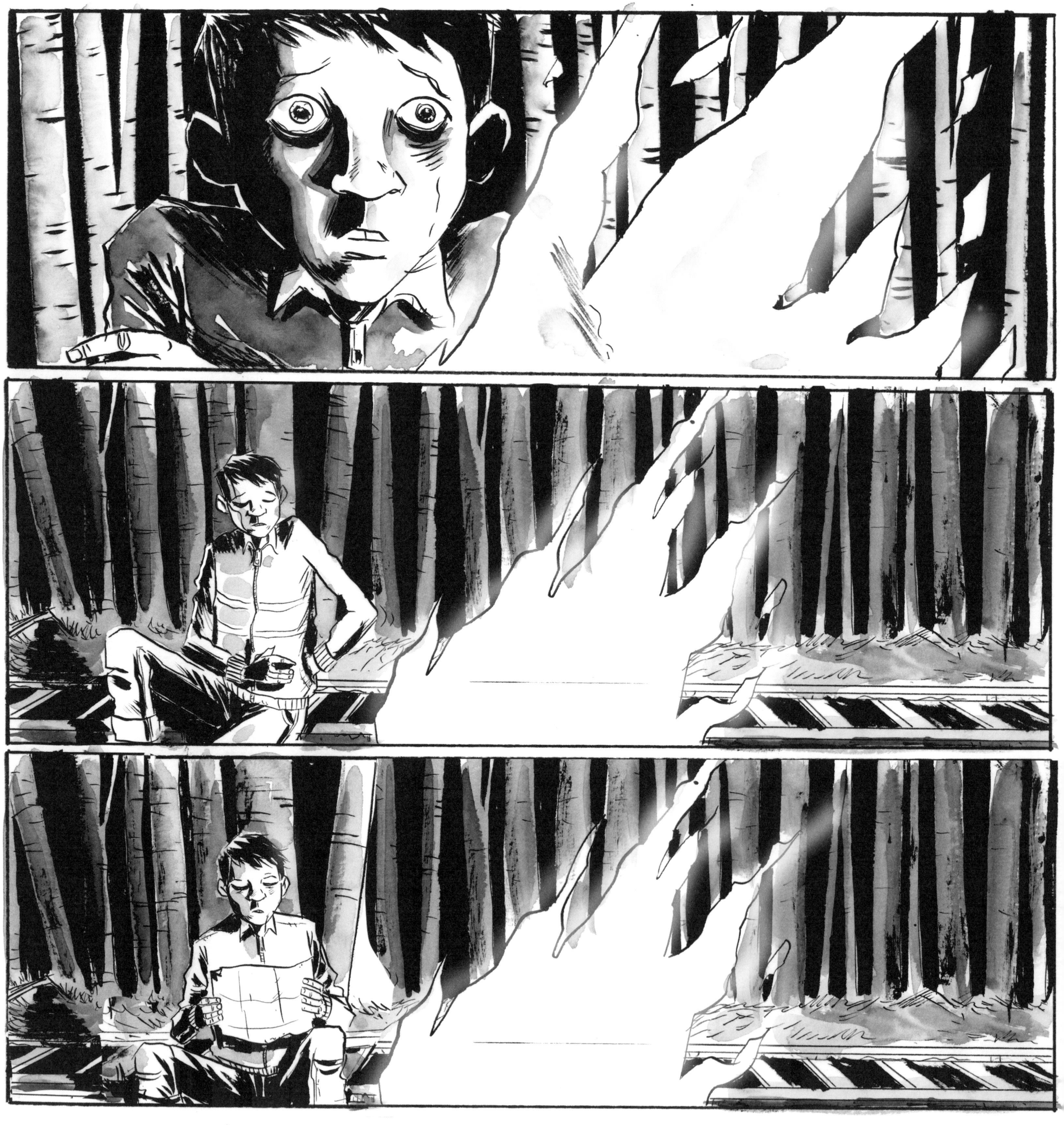

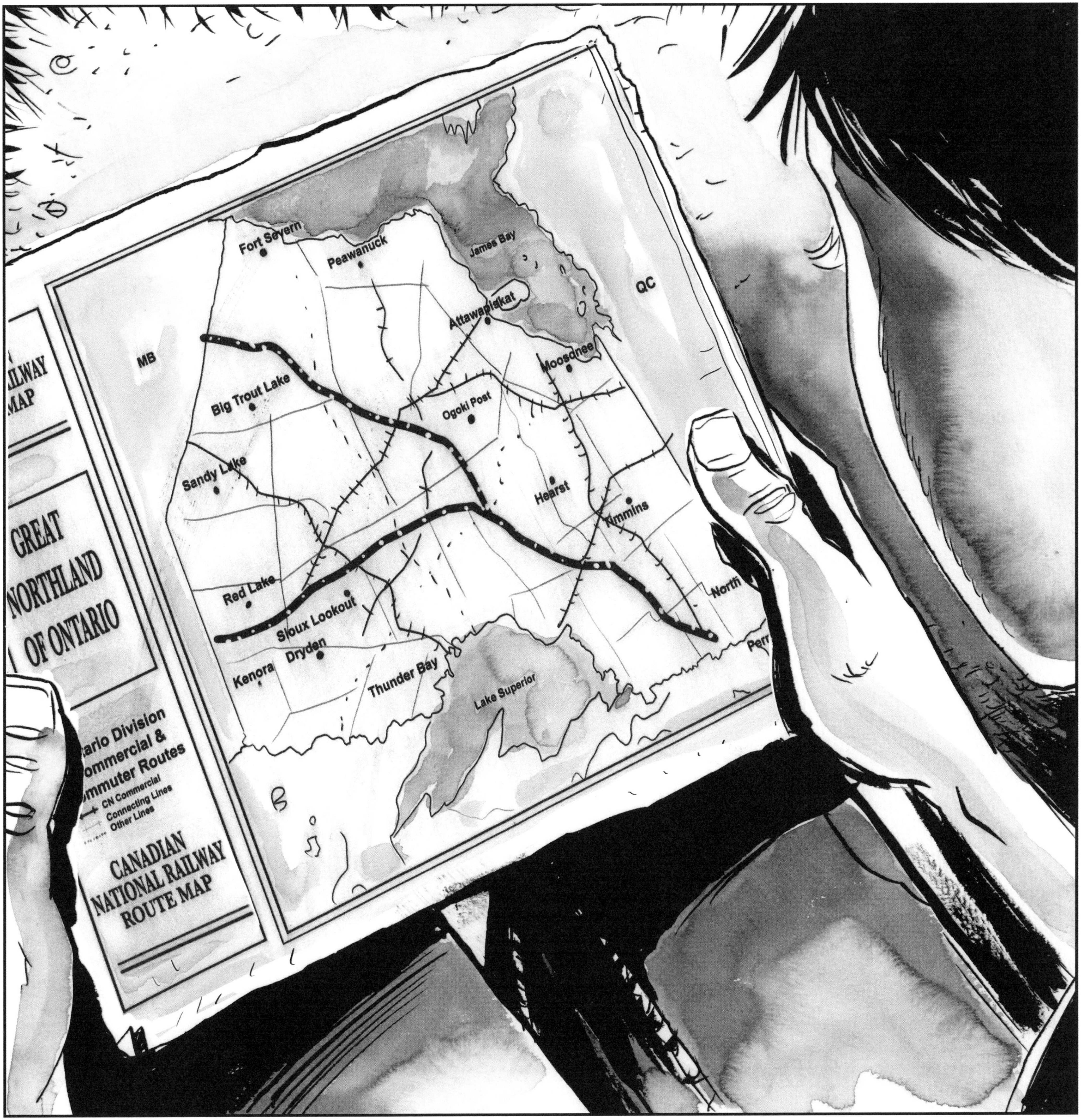
ILWAY
MAP
GREAT
NORTHLAND
OF ONTARIO
tario Division
ommercial &
mmuter Routes
CN Commercial
Connecting Lines
Other Lines
CANADIAN
NATIONAL RAILWAY
ROUTE MAP
Fort Severn
Peawanuck
James Bay
QC
Attawapiskat
MB
Moosonee
Big Trout Lake
Ogoki Post
Sandy Lake
Hearst
Timmins
Red Lake
Sioux Lookout
North
Dryden
Kenora
Thunder Bay
Perr
Lake Superior

Red Lake
Sioux Lookout
Kenora
Dryden
Hearst
Timmins
4+6=10
4+7=11
DOG — SEE THE DOG RUN
CAT — SEE THE CAT
MAN — SEE THE MAN
BOY — SEE THE BOY RUN
SEE
RUN

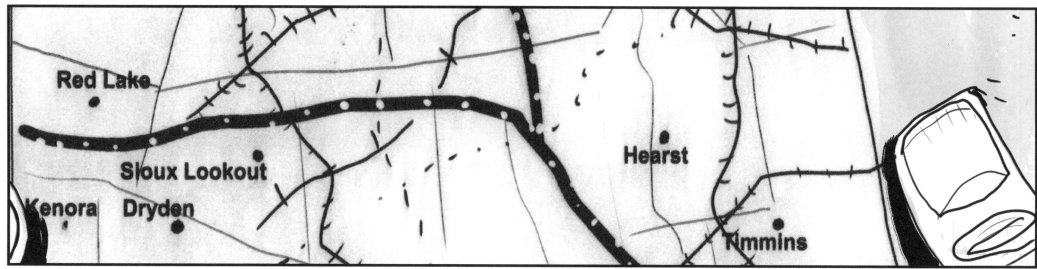

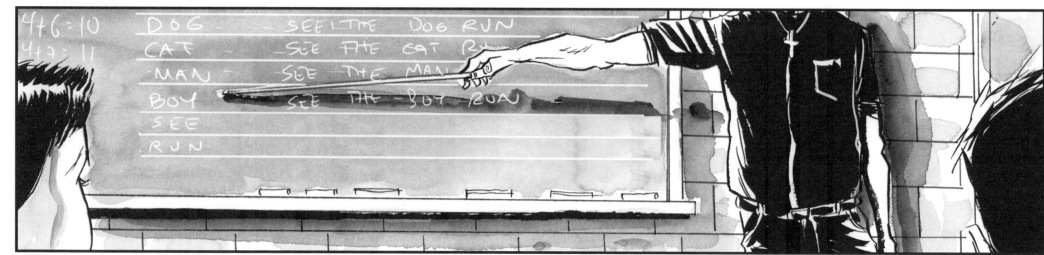

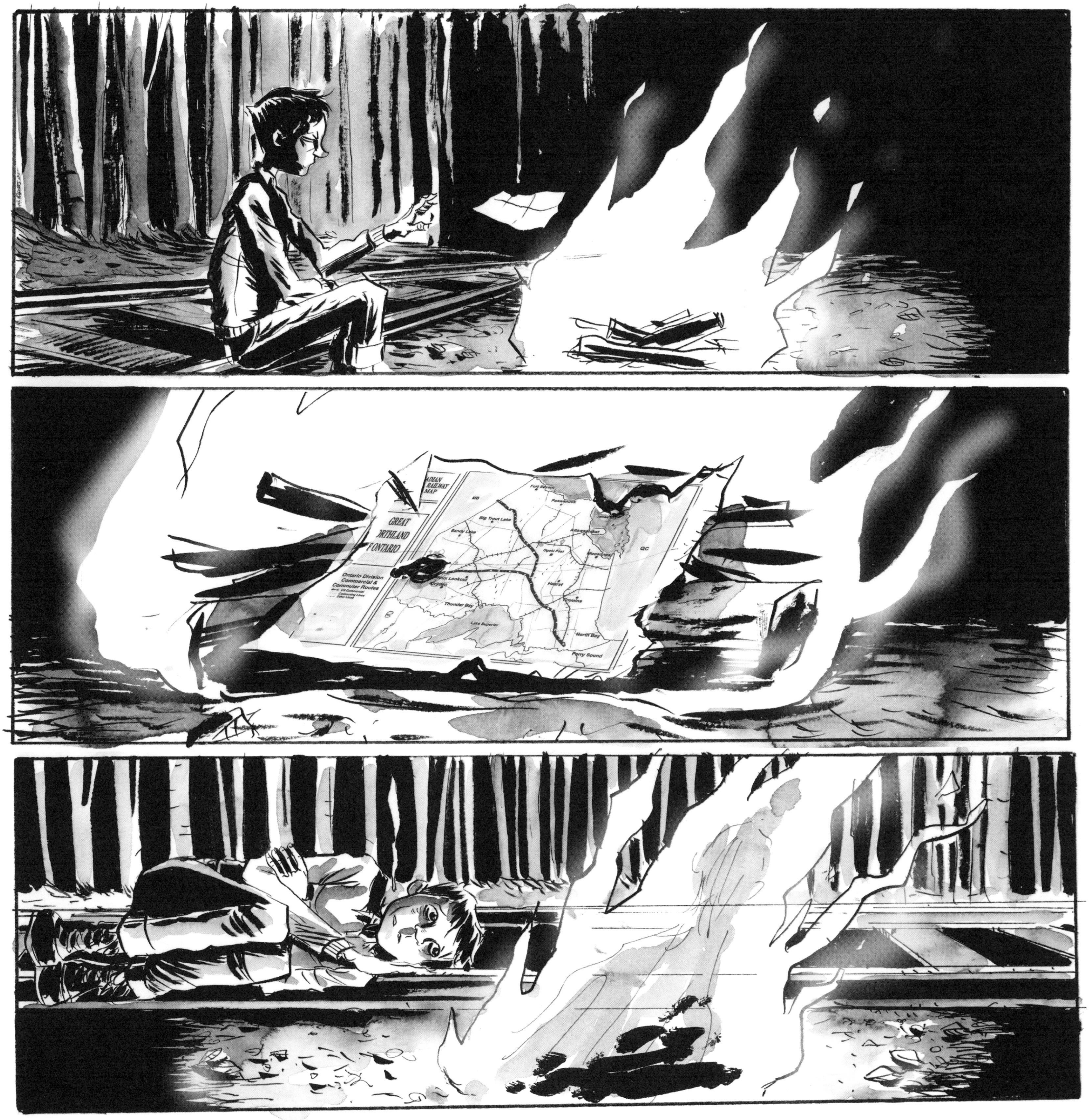
ADIAN
RAILWAY
MAP
GREAT
ORTHLAND
F ONTARIO
Ontario Division
Commercial &
Commuter Routes
MB
Fort Severn
Peawanuck
Big Trout Lake
Sandy Lake
Ogoki Post
Moosonee
QC
Hearst
Dryden
Thunder Bay
Timmins
Lake Superior
North Bay
Perry Sound

SON

You know that they just can't resist
No man could make them feel nervous
And they put zero into it
And their country doesn't exist

Son, when you dance
I'll be on your shoulder
And you'll feel it

Son, when you dance
I'll be on your shoulder
And you'll feel it

And when something stirs in your heart
A feeling so strong and intense
When something occurs in your heart
And there isn't a next sentence

Son, when you dance
I'll be on your shoulder
And you'll feel it

Even as the world convulses
Don't stop wishing what you wish
Even as the world convulses
Even as the world convulses
Don't stop wishing the things you wish
Don't stop wishing what you wish

And when something stirs in your heart
A feeling so strong and intense
When something occurs in your heart
And there isn't a next sentence.

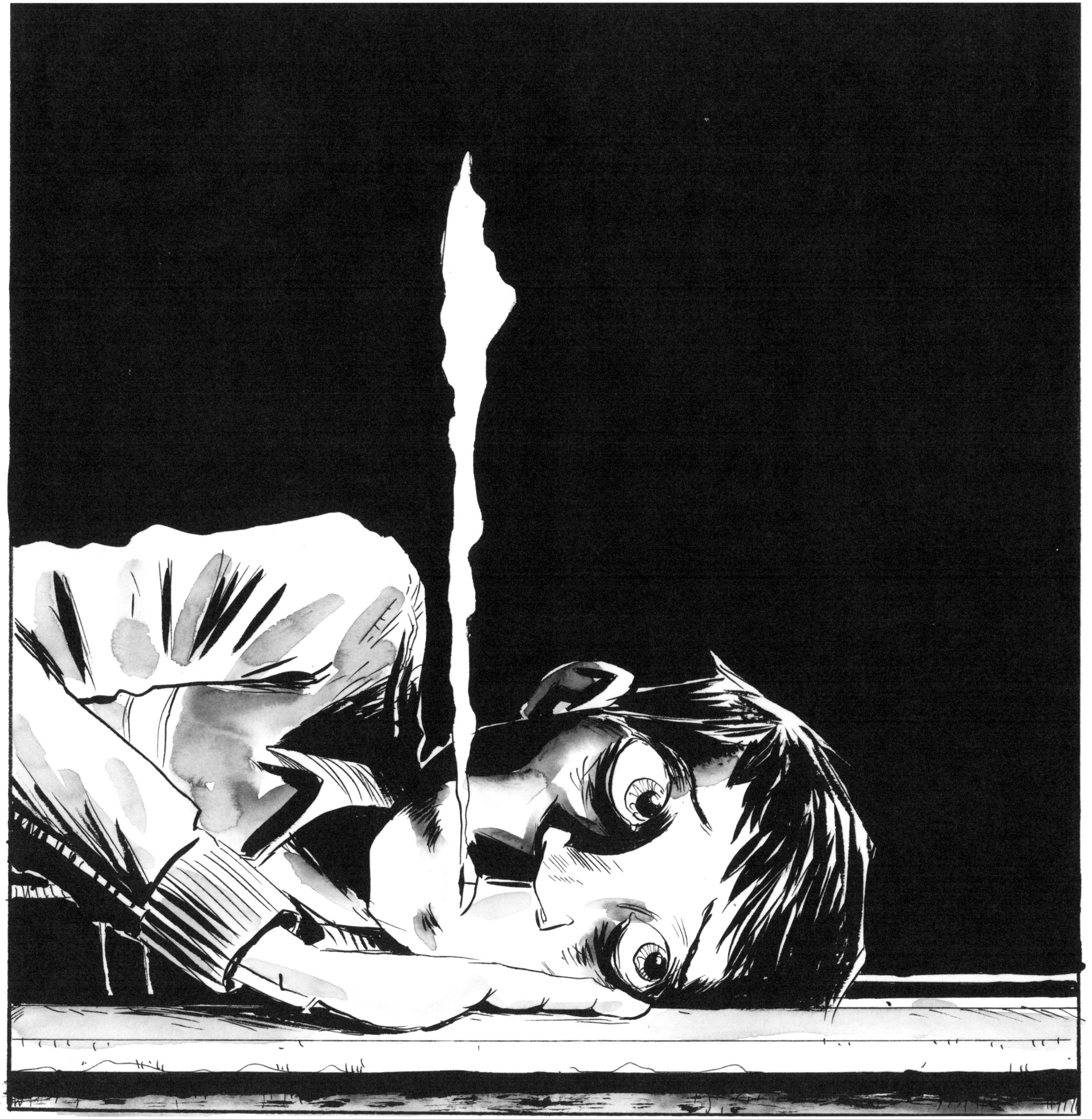

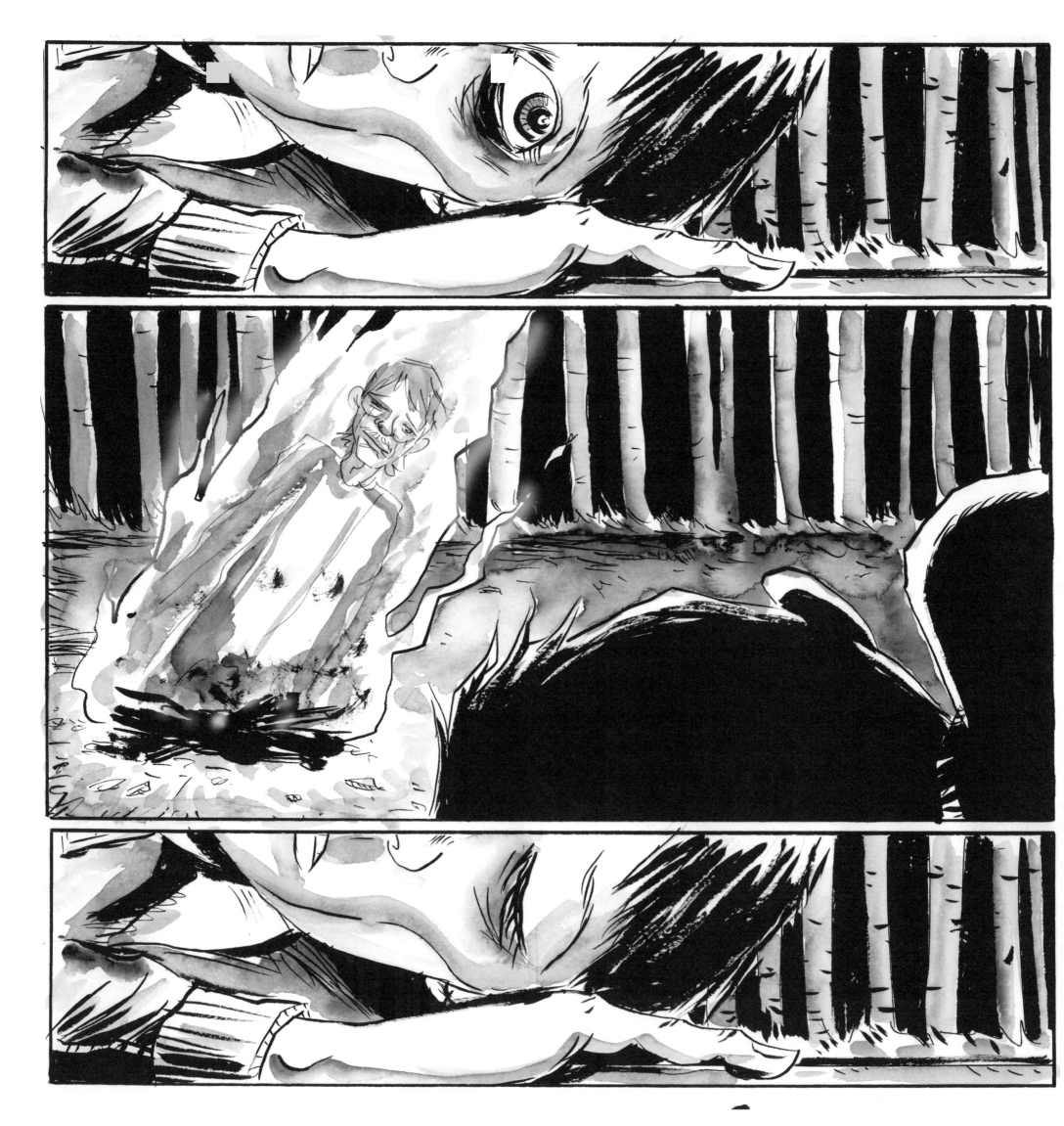

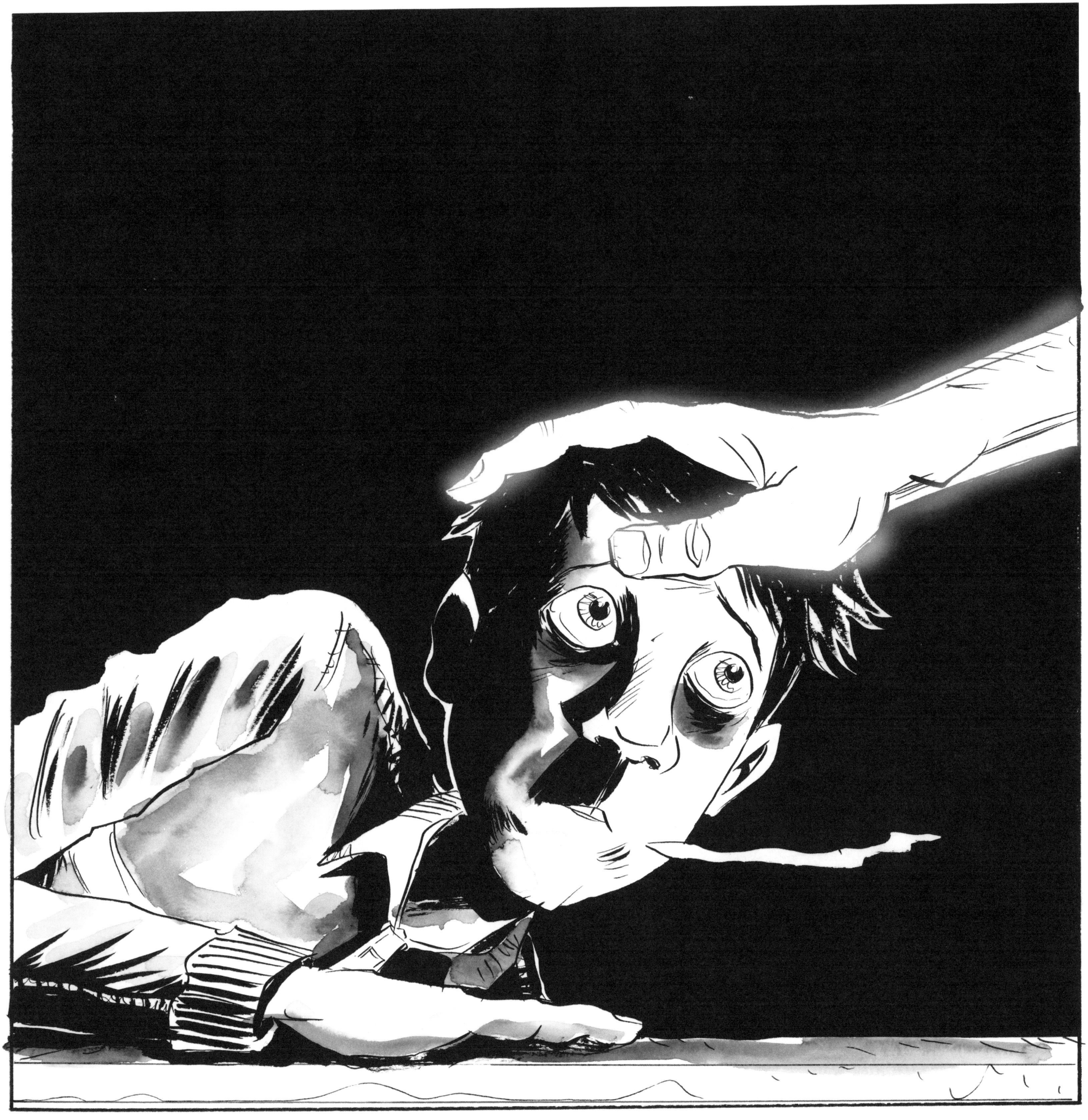

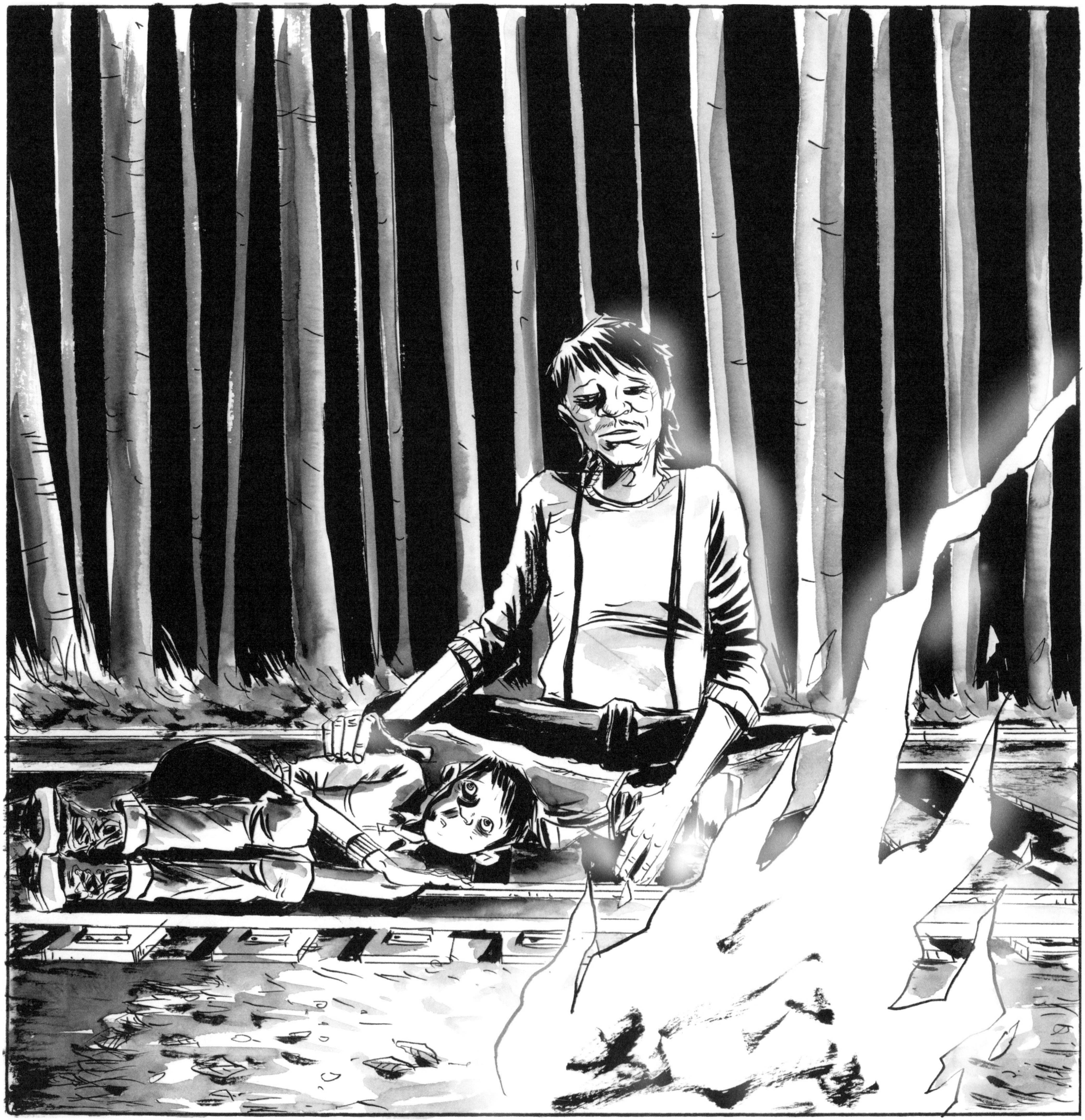

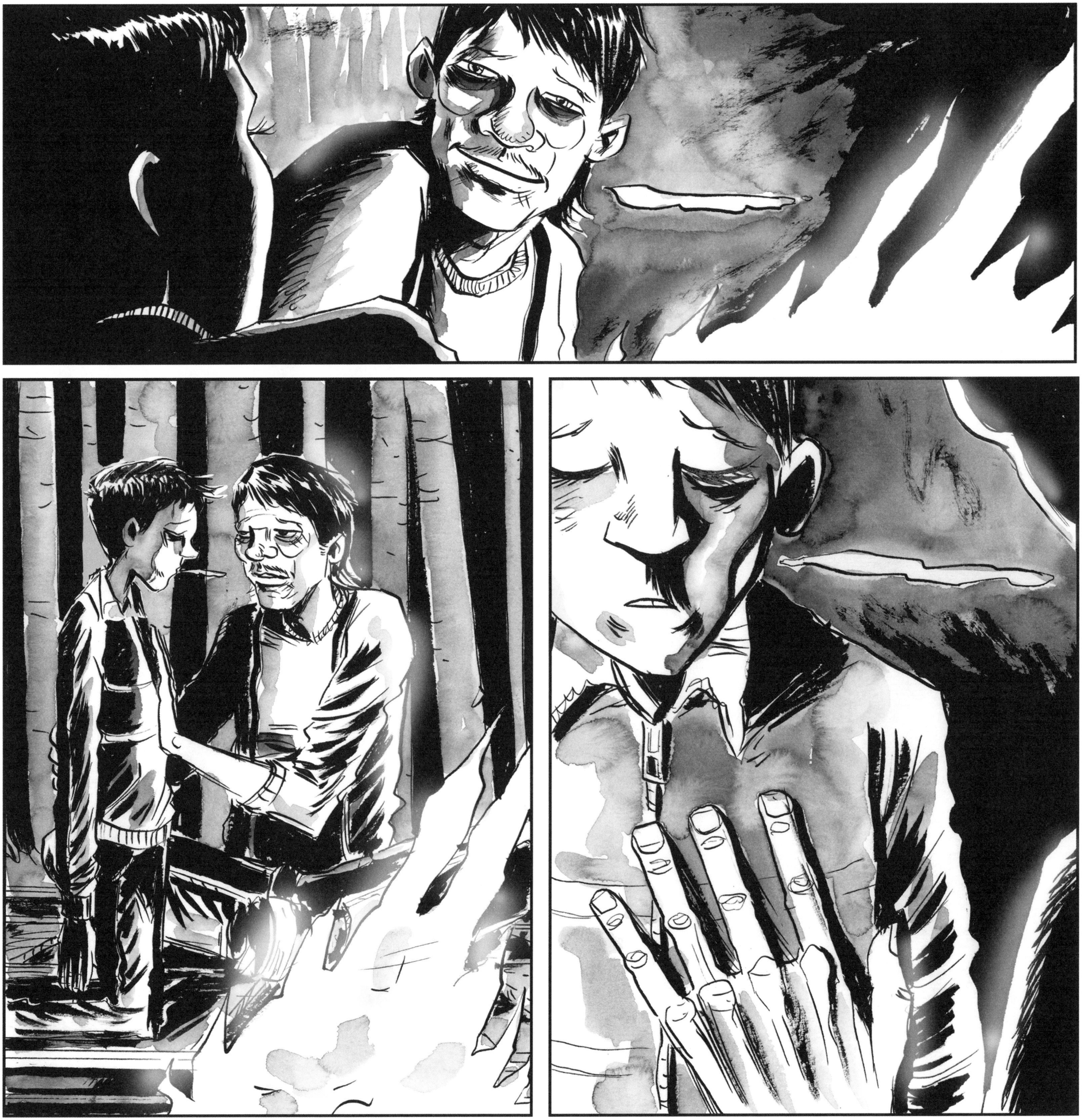

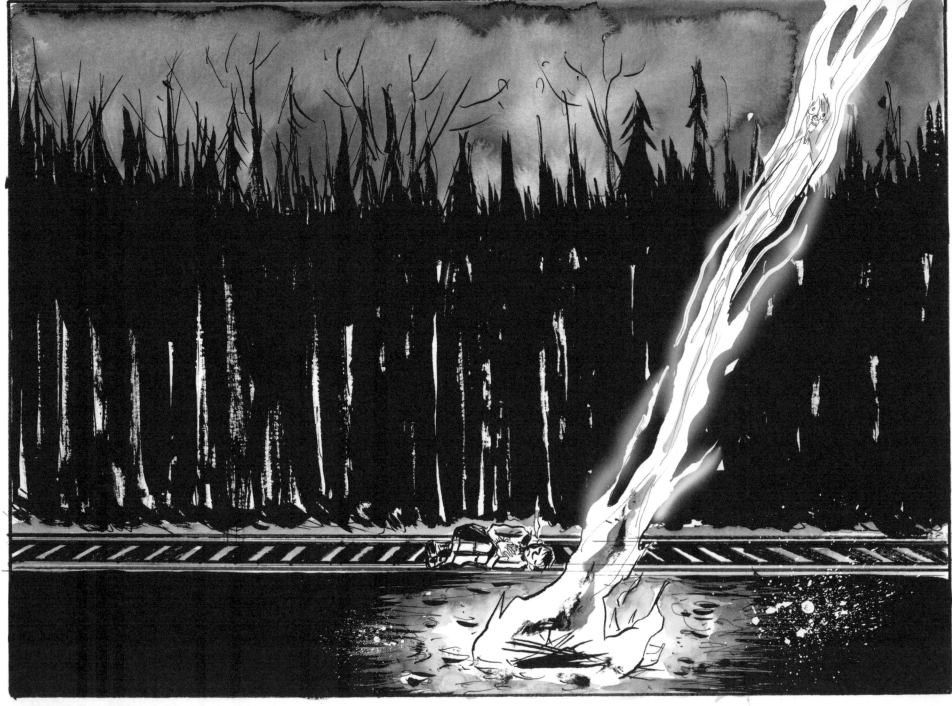

SECRET PATH

Freezing rain
And ice pellets
Walking home
I'm covered in it

Walking home
Along the tracks
Secret Path
Did you say "Secret Path"?

Pale blue
Doesn't do what they said it'd do
It's just a jacket
It's a windbreaker
It's not a jean jacket
They call it a windbreaker

Walking home
Along the tracks
Secret Path
He said, "Secret Path"

I am soaked
To the skin
There's never been
A colder rain than this one I'm in

Pale blue
Doesn't do what they said it'd do
It's not my jacket
It's a windbreaker
It's not my jean jacket
It's just a windbreaker

And the fuck-off rocks
Along the tracks
Secret Path
There's no "Secret Path"

And the freezing rain
And the ice pellets
Coat the rail
So I can't even tightrope it.

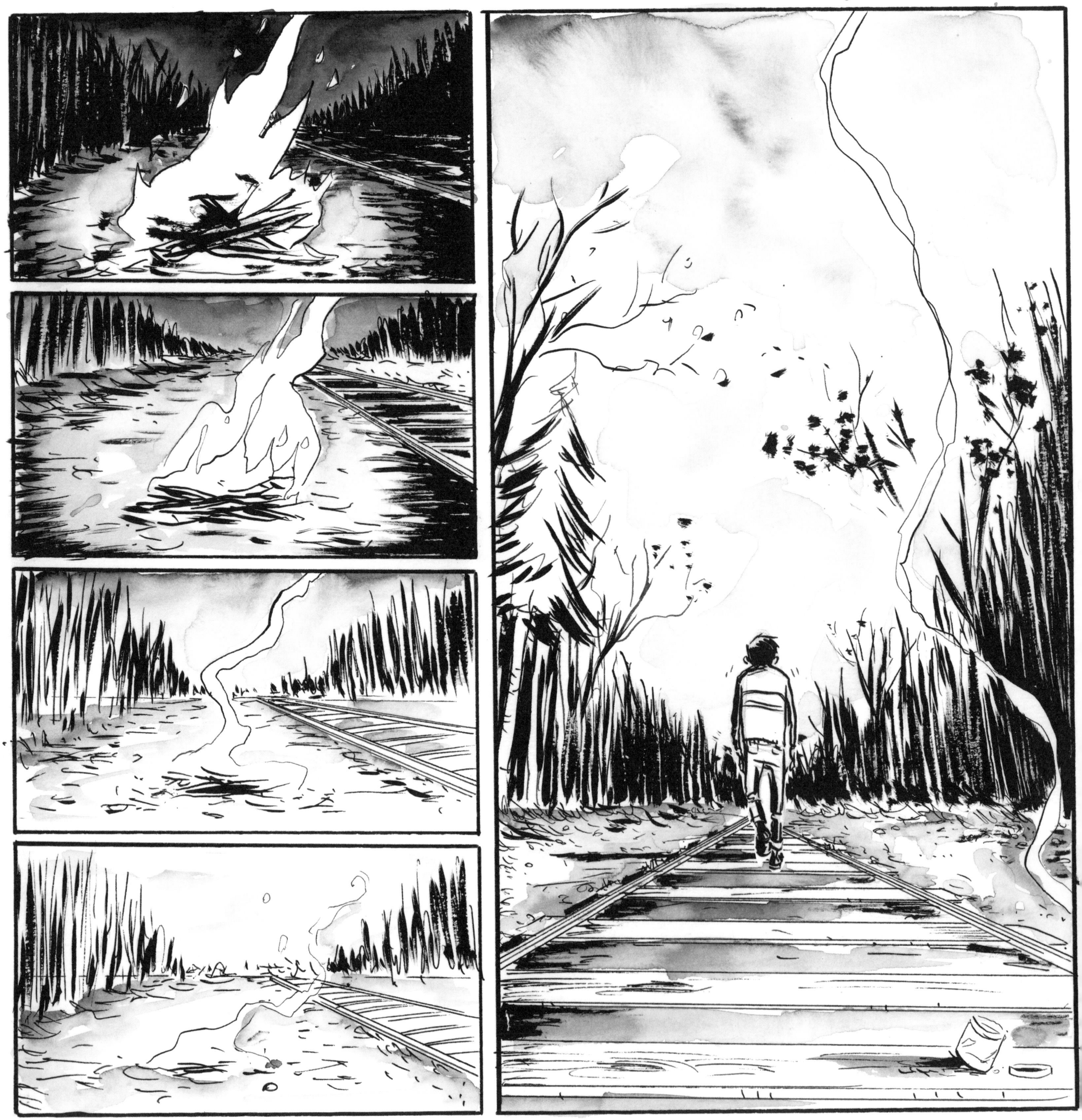

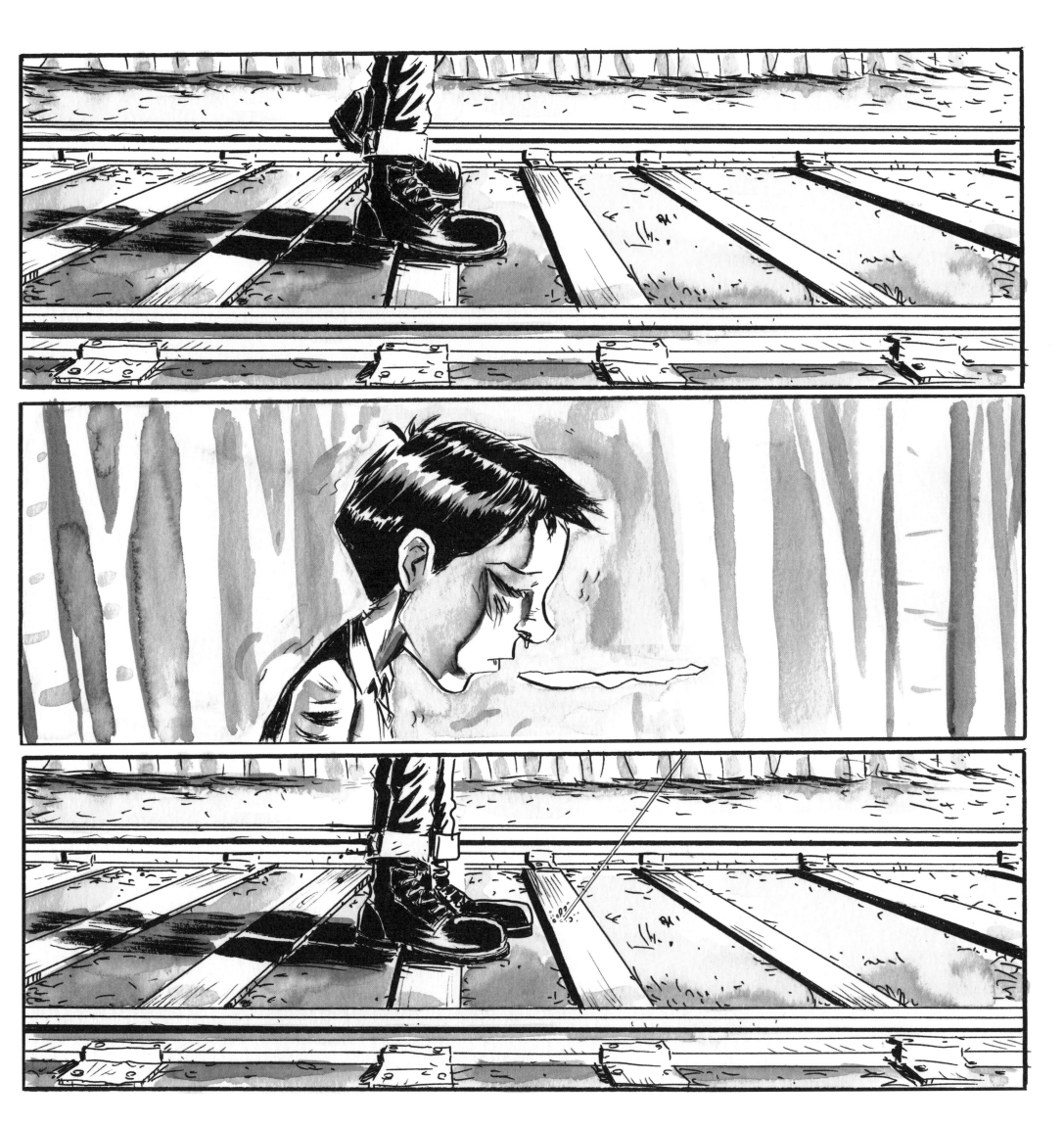

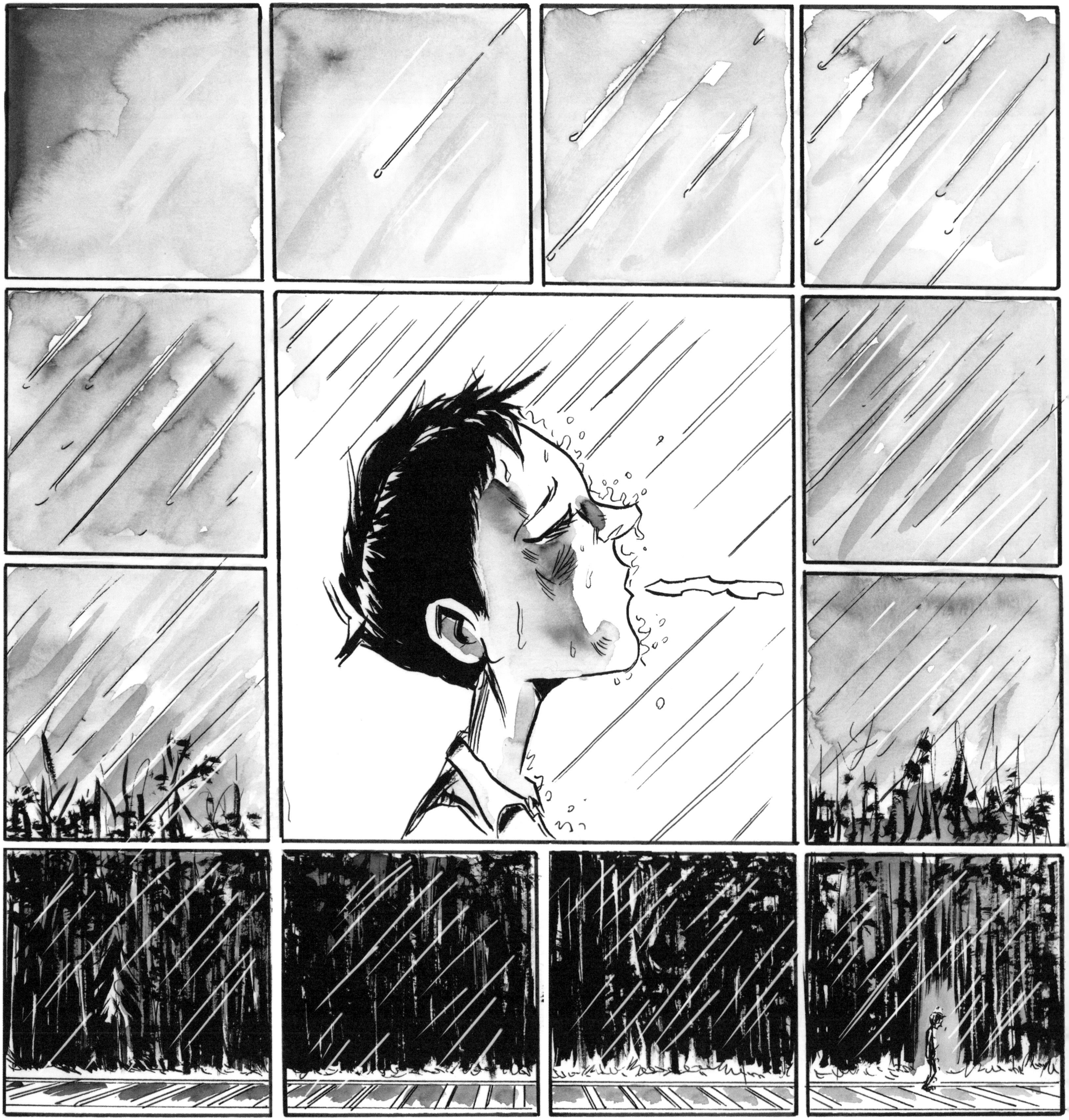

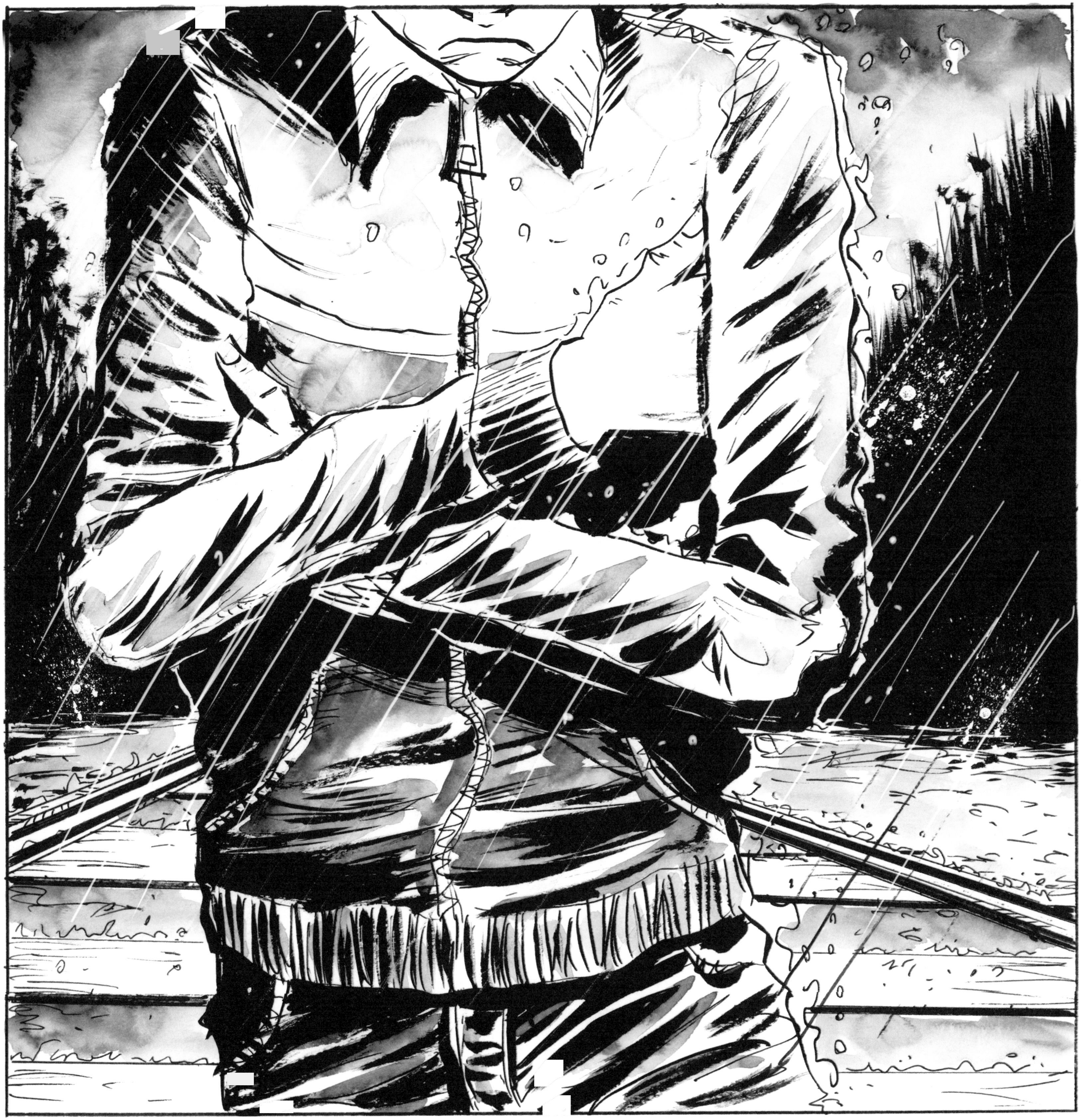

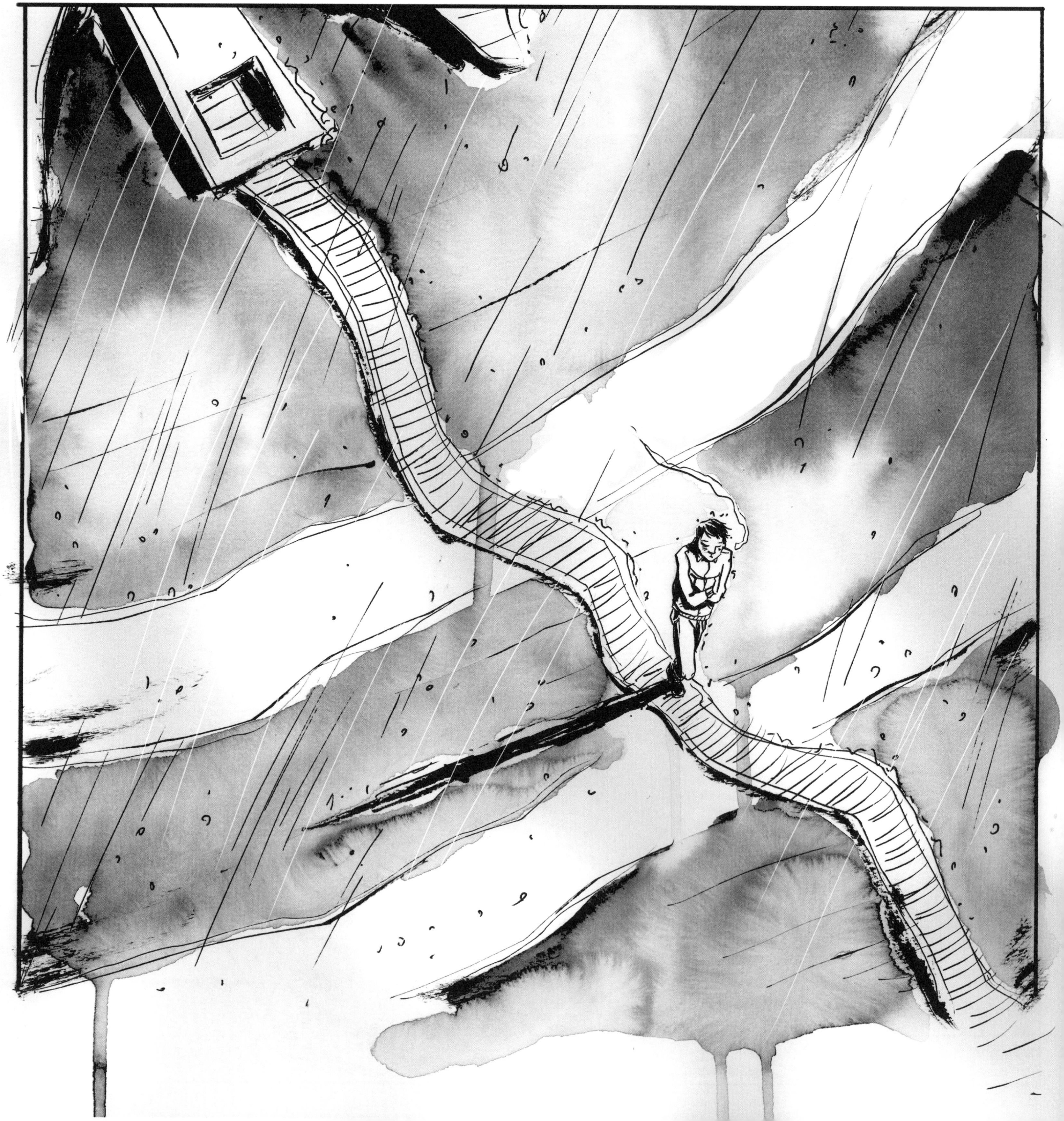

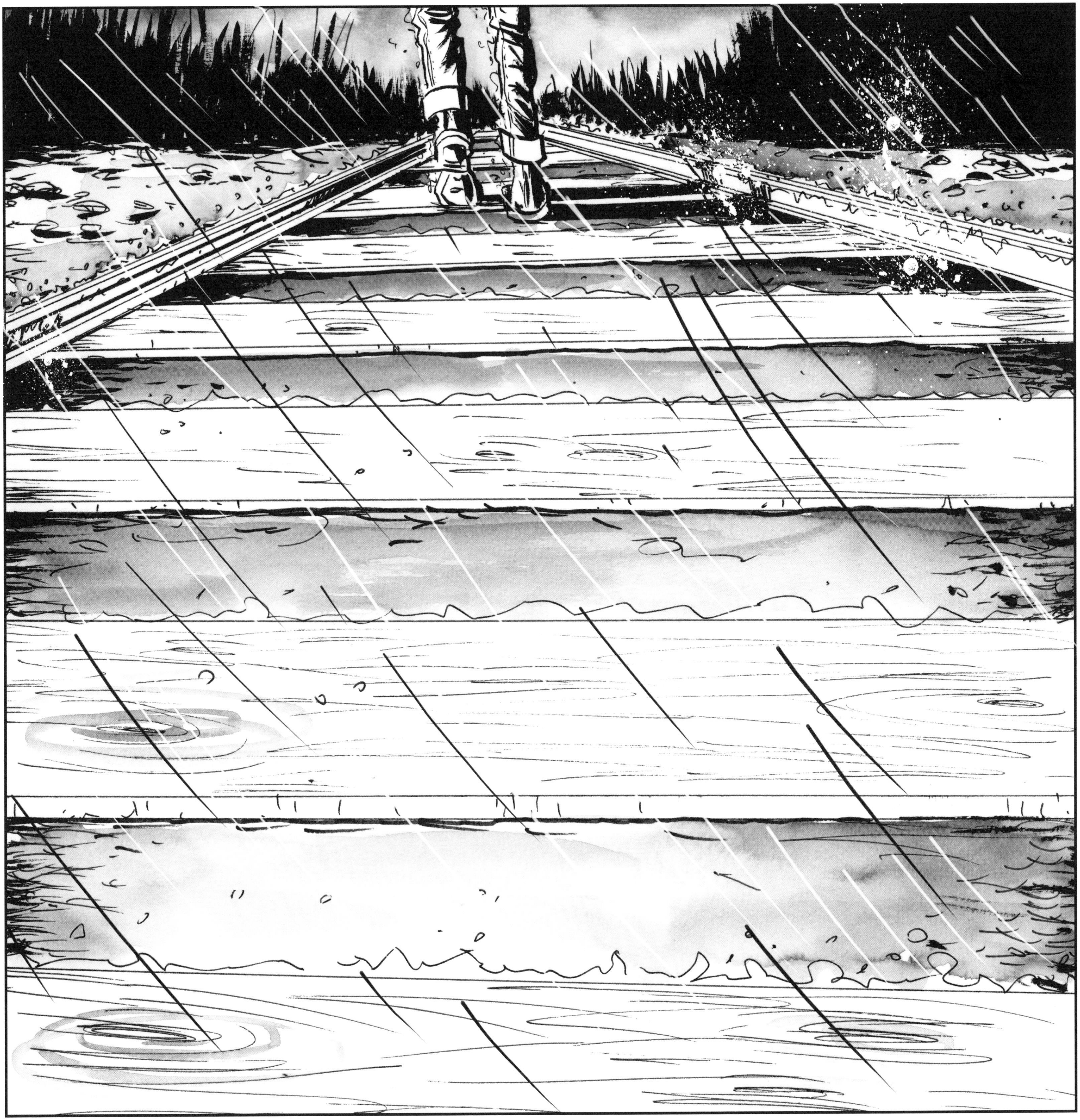

DON'T LET THIS TOUCH YOU

Don't let this touch you
Don't let this touch you

Words are birds
Words are snow
Words whisper
Words don't make the rain go

Wilderness
Can't be done
Unfinished
Can't be done

Don't let it touch you
Don't let this touch you

Words are blanks
Words are ghosts
Words are god
Words don't make the rain go

I'm confused by freedom
What do you do with freedom?

I heard them in the dark
Heard the things they do
I heard the heavy whispers
Whispering, "Don't let this touch you."

Don't let this touch you
            Don't
Don't let it touch you
            Don't

His glowing face
By the stove
His orange face
Daddy, make the rain go.

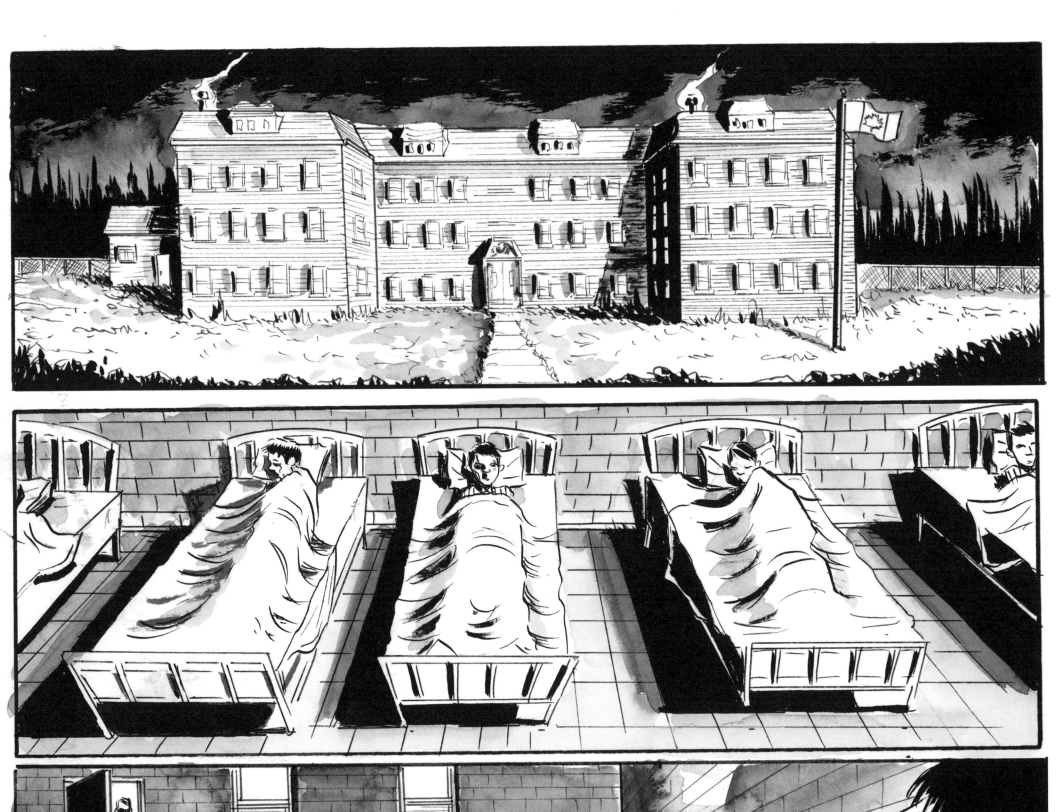

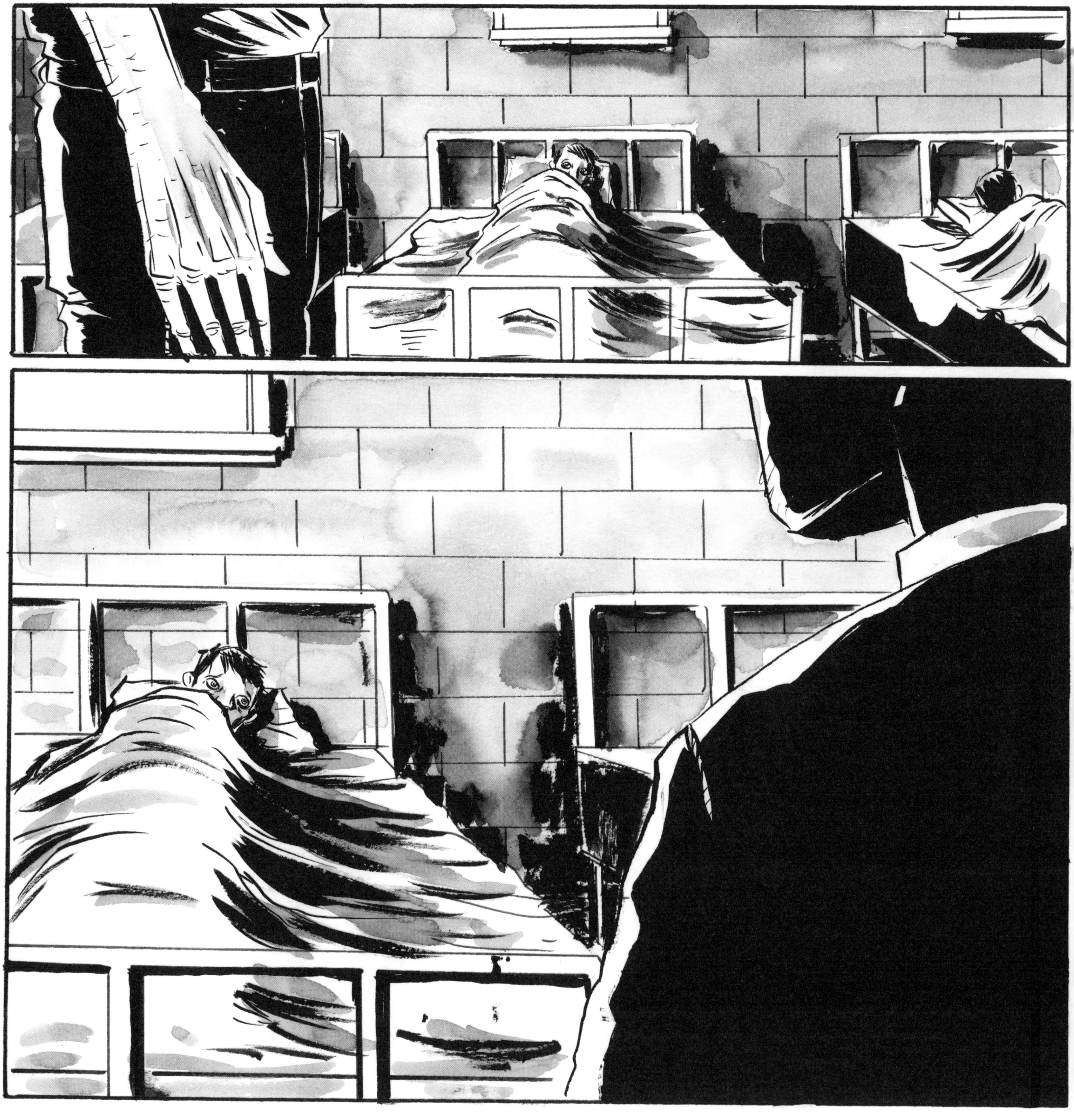

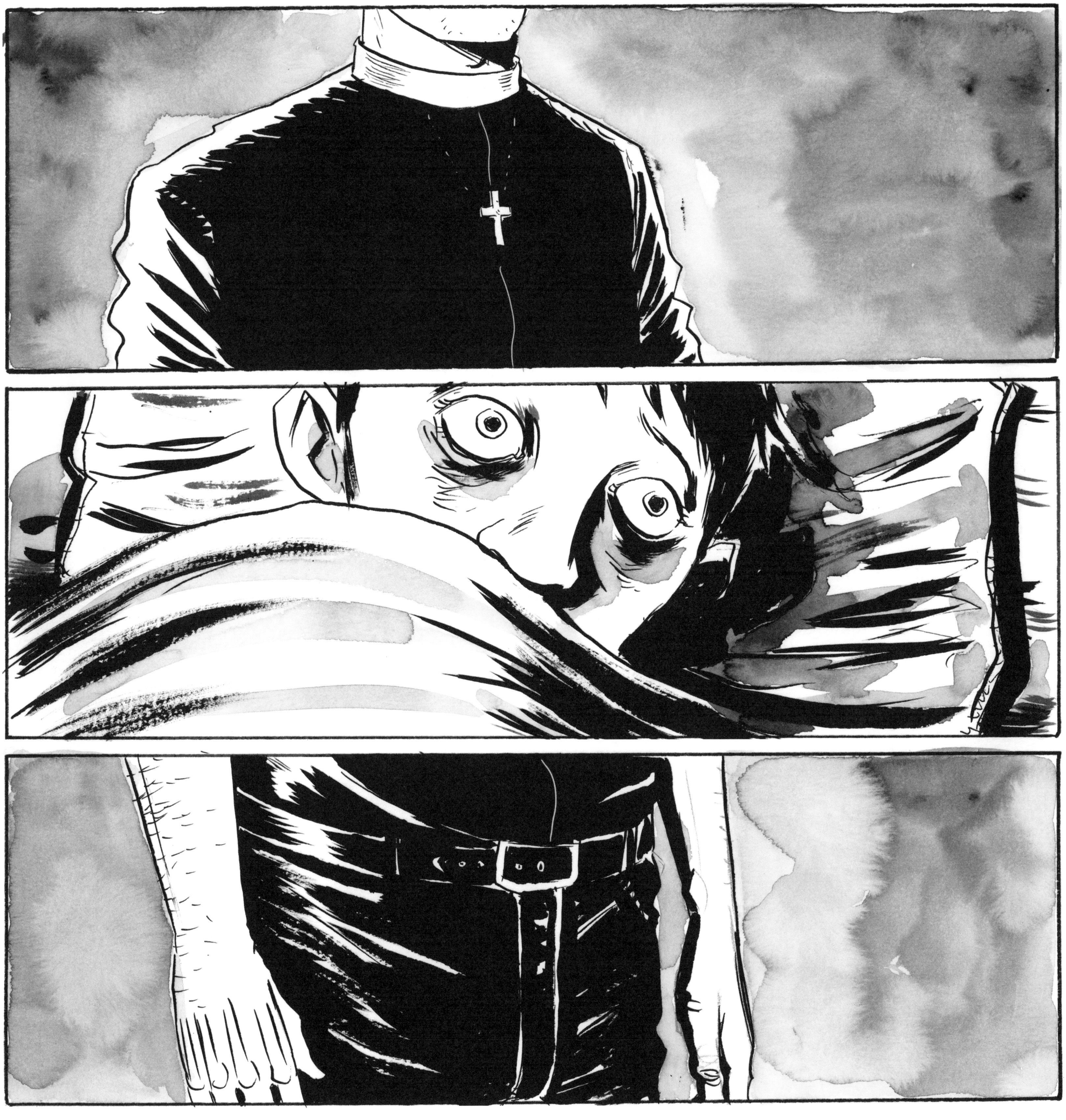

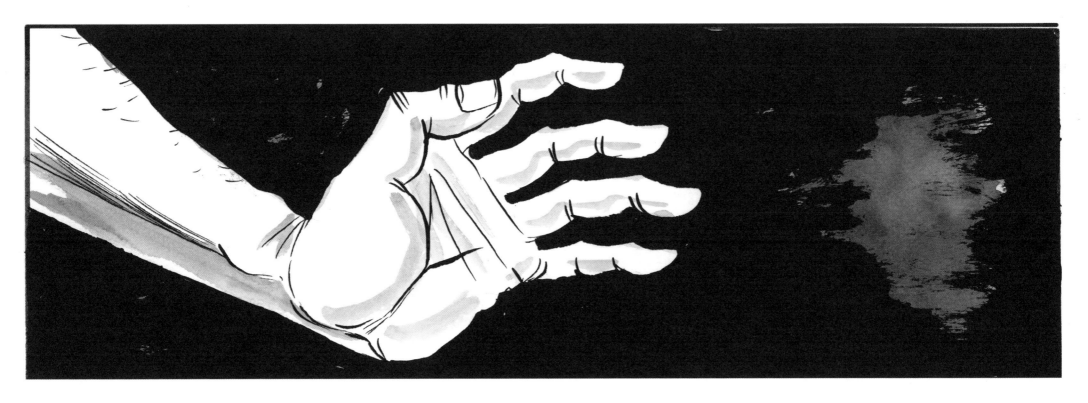

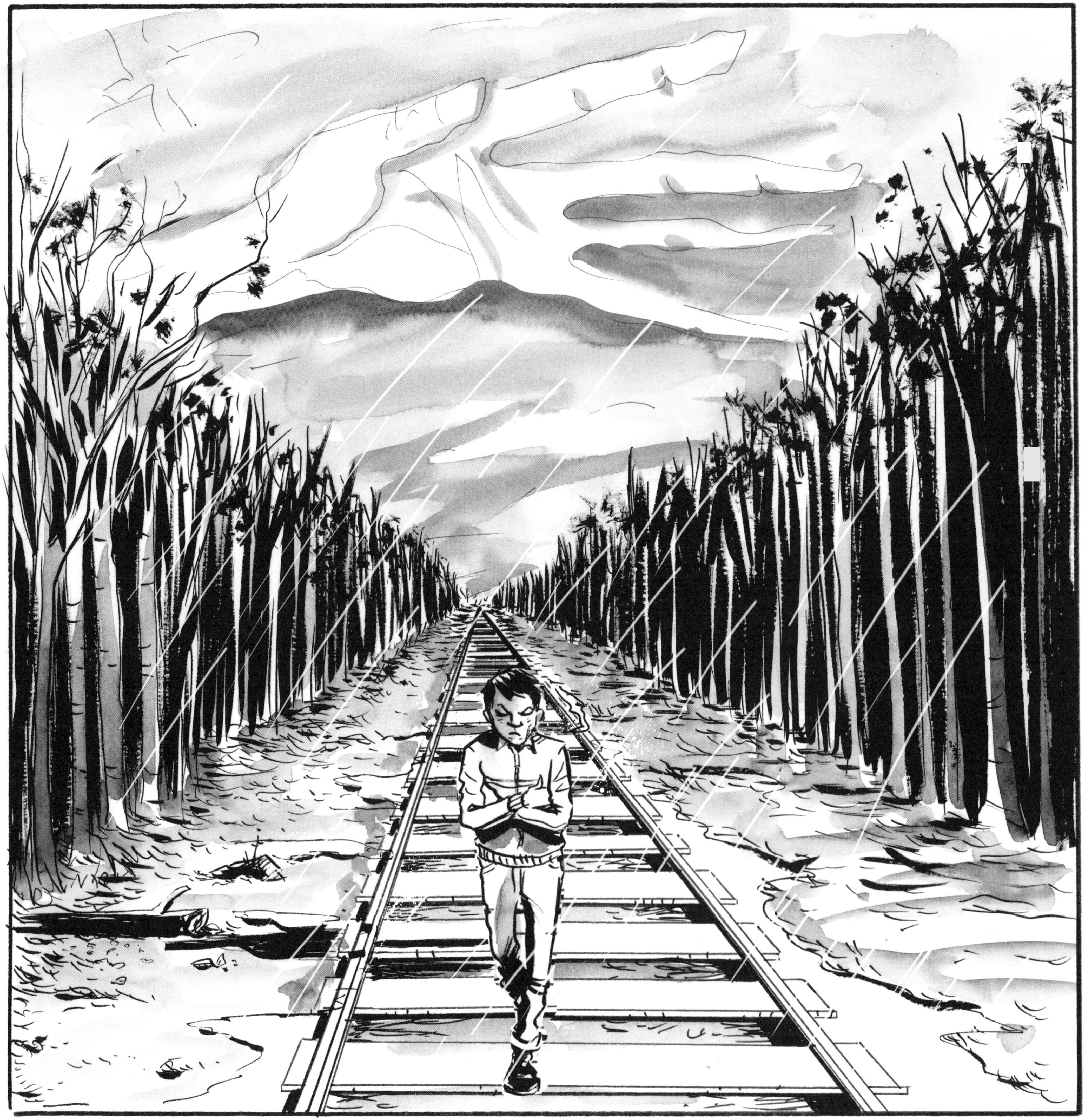

HAUNT THEM, HAUNT THEM, HAUNT THEM

I think I'm in despair
The wind is in the trees
Basically just waiting for something to come along and eat me

Is this future's gate?
Where my dreams retreat?
And all of memories are just memories of memories?

And enfolded in a dream
Pitch-black and glowing blue
A raven saying, "I know a way that I can help you."

I stared into his eyes
I saw my pale last days
He said, "What you can't escape, you gotta embrace."

I know a way to get back
This don't have to end
A way to get back
And haunt them, haunt them, haunt them

Then he wished me plain
As he flew away
Said I'd see him coming on that pale last day

And he wished me plain
Ordinary death
Said he'd be back after I escaped it

I've seen how they are
How they'd all sell their souls
In little bits and pieces till they get old
You don't make a dent
In indifference
Ya gotta haunt them, haunt them, haunt them

But I want to go back
If this is the end
I want to go back
Not to haunt them, haunt them, haunt them

Not to haunt them, haunt them, haunt them
Not to haunt them, haunt them, haunt them
Haunt them. Haunt them. Haunt them.

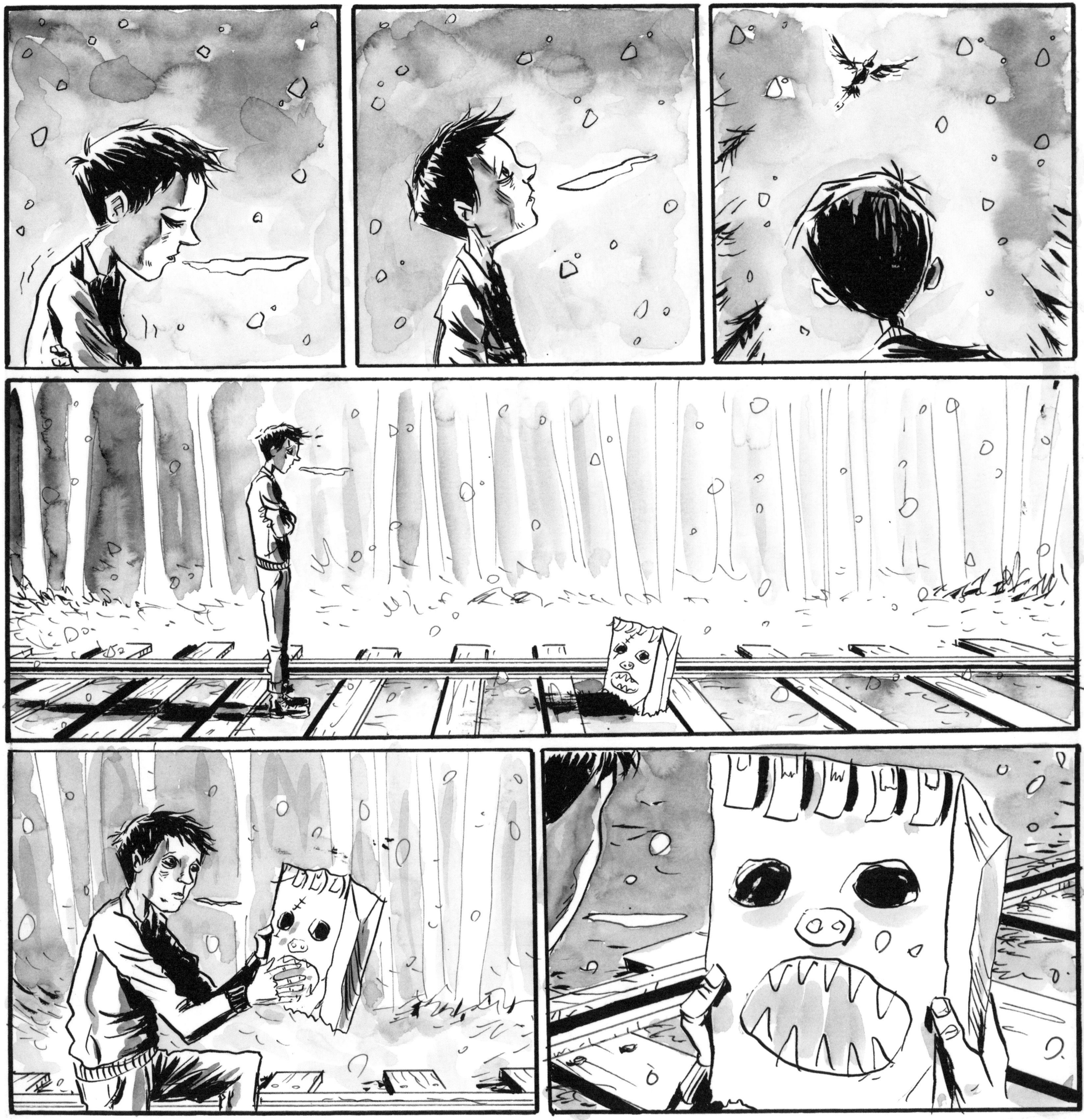

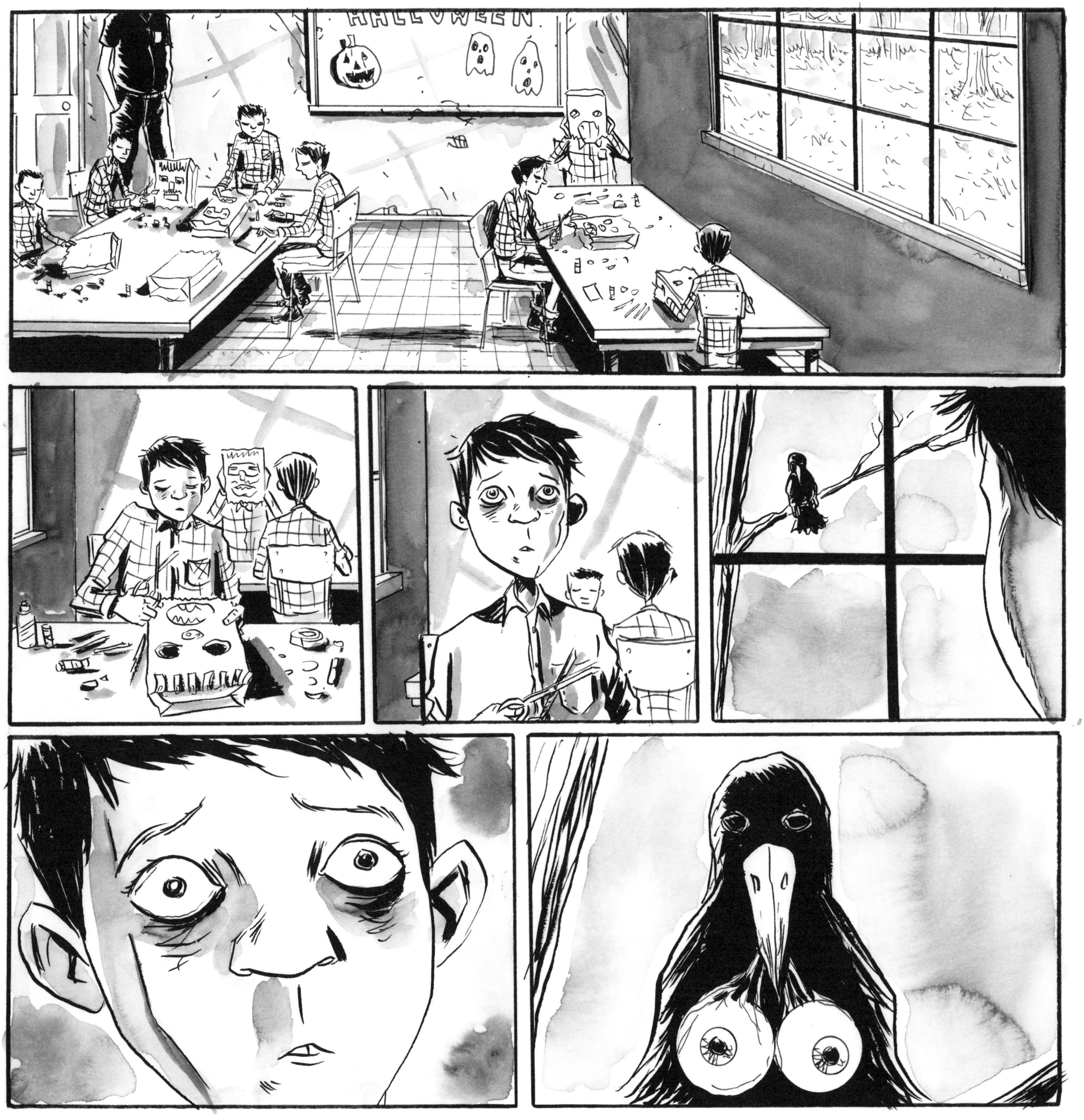
HALLOWEEN

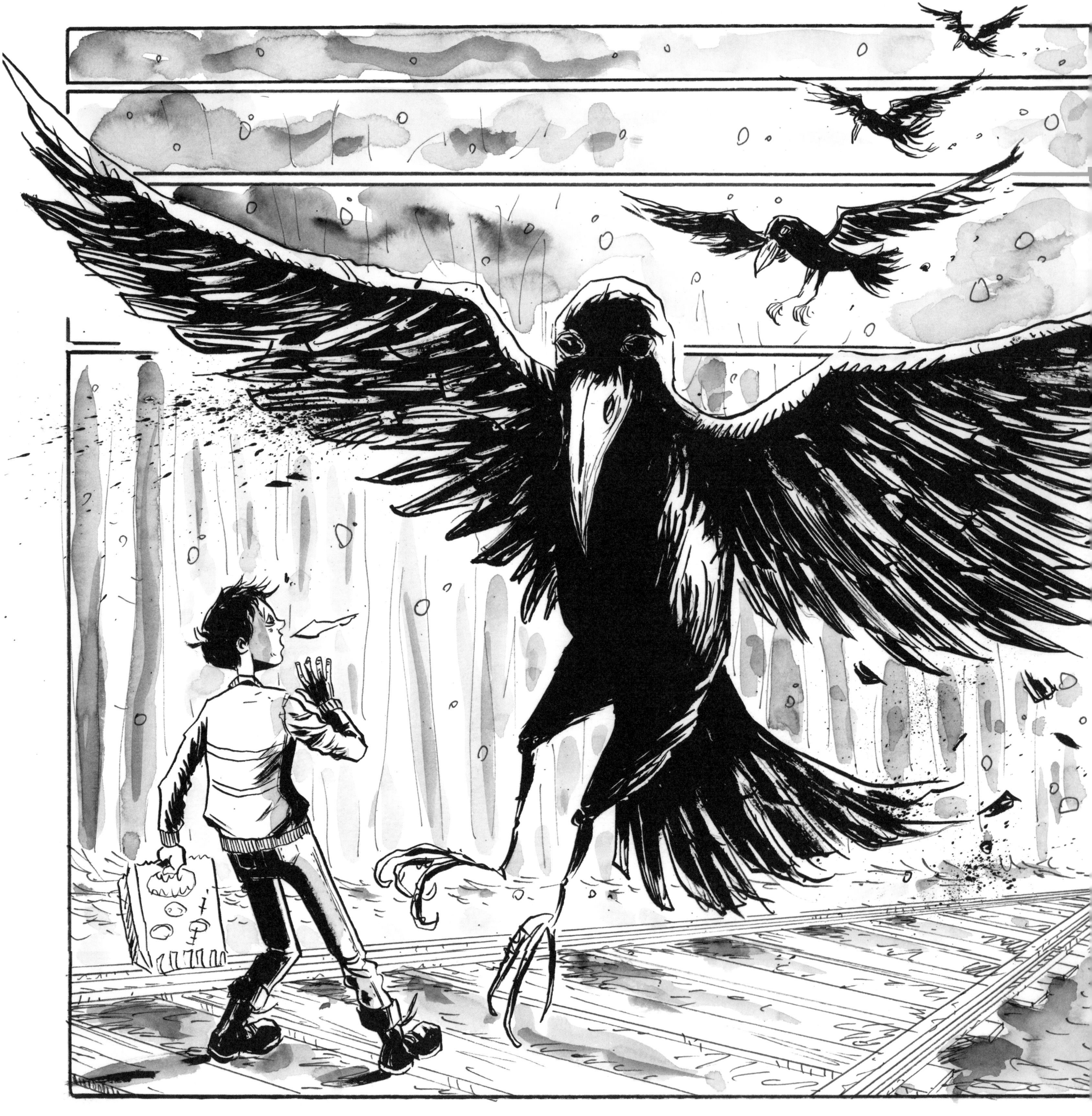

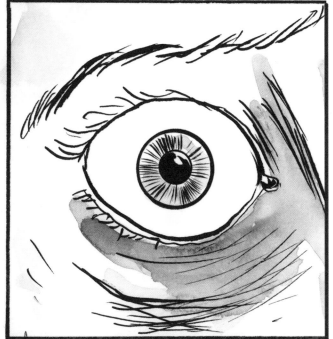

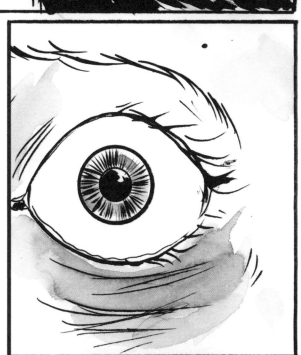

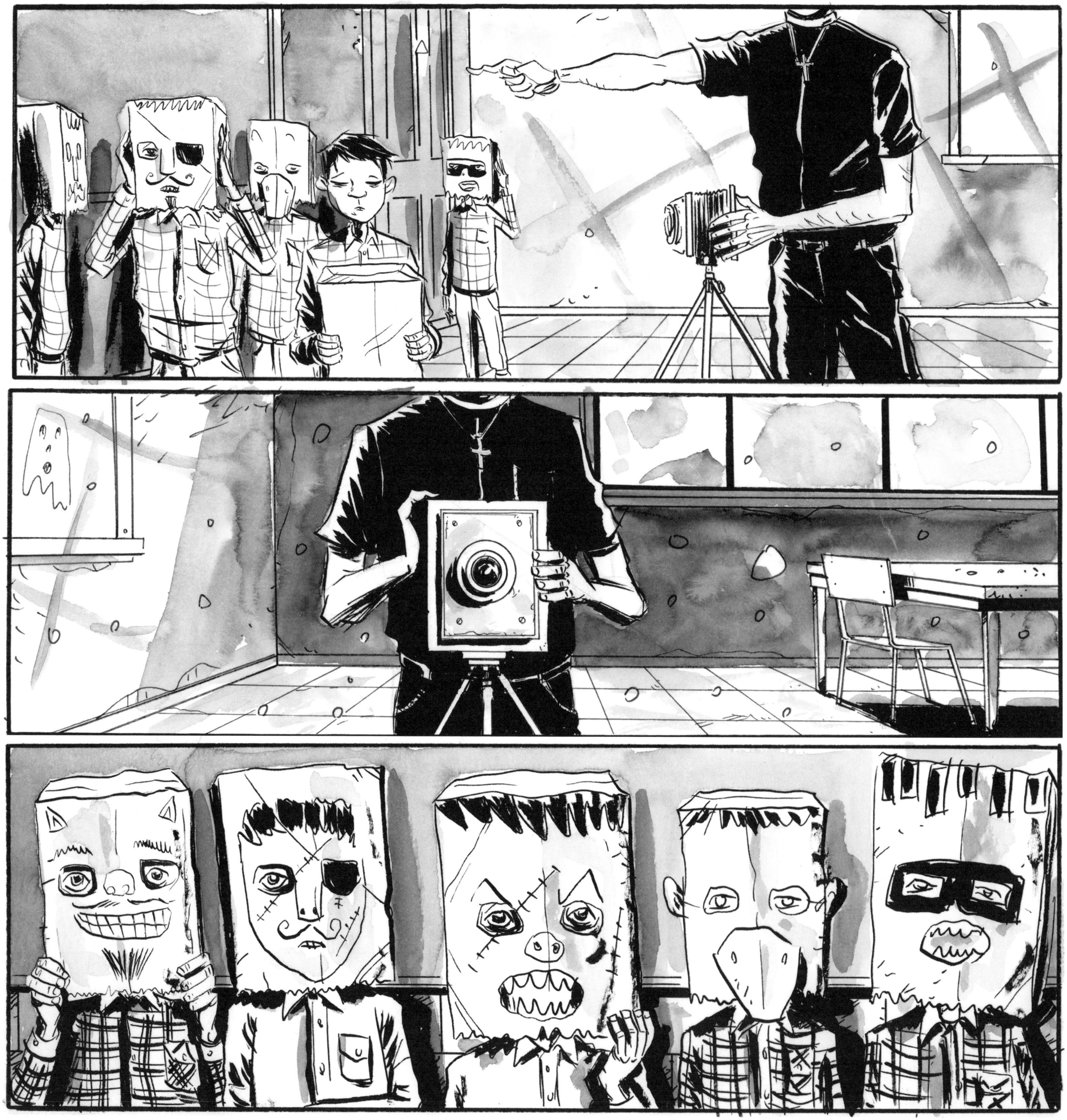

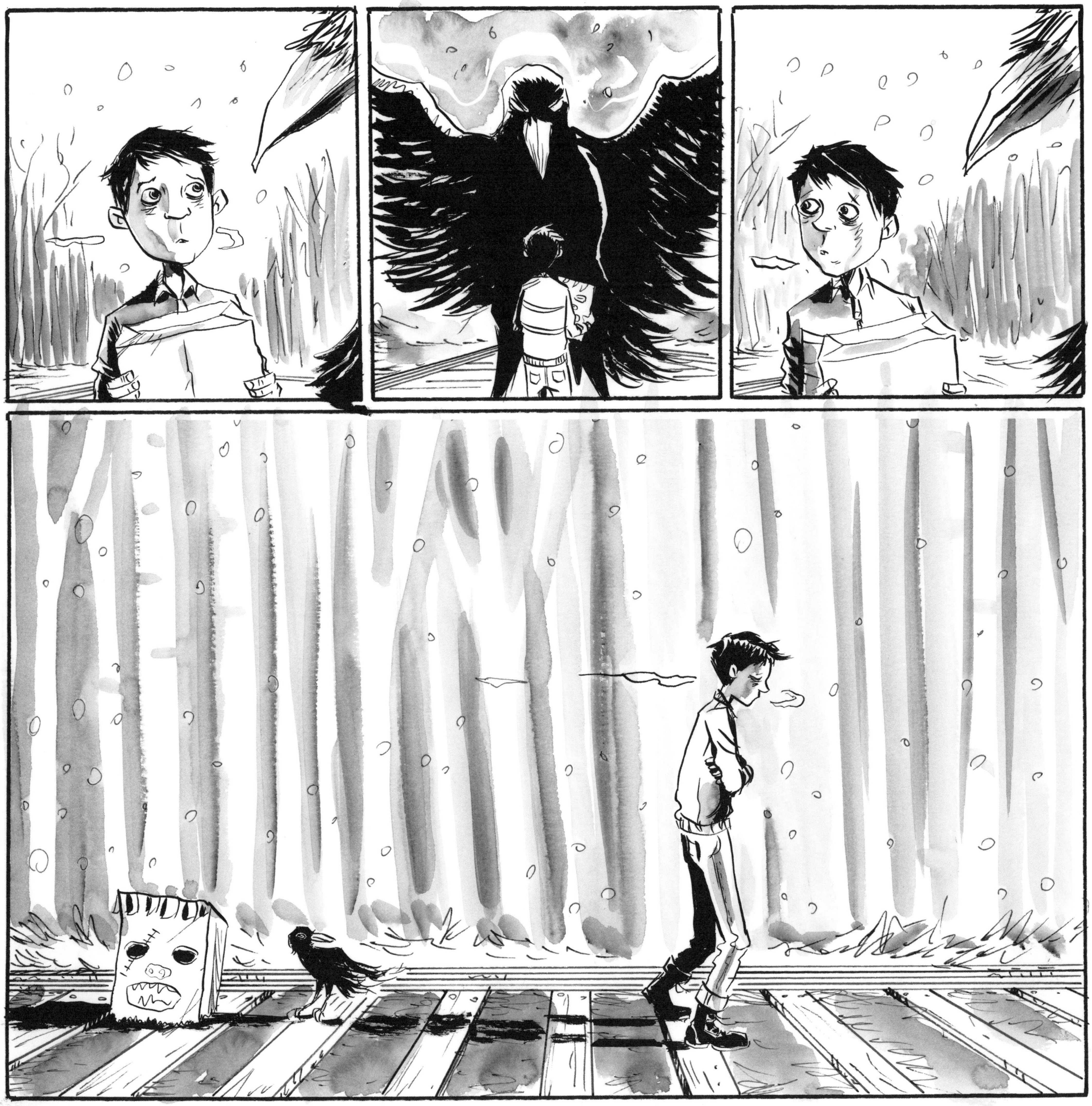

THE ONLY PLACE TO BE

I'll just close my eyes
I'll just catch my breath
This is the only place to be
I've got lots of time
My whole life ahead
This is the only place to be

It's a earthlike world
As cold and real
With a sunlike star
You can feel

I am for the wolf
Pitch-black and yellow eyes
This is the only place to be
For the raven arriving
First to get my eyes
This is the only place to be
And I'm for the poor sun
Always against the mindless night
This is the only place to be
I am for the wind
In the pale blue sky
This is the only place to be

On this earthlike world
It's cold and real
With a sunlike star
You can feel

I'll just close my eyes
I'll just catch my breath
This is the only place to be

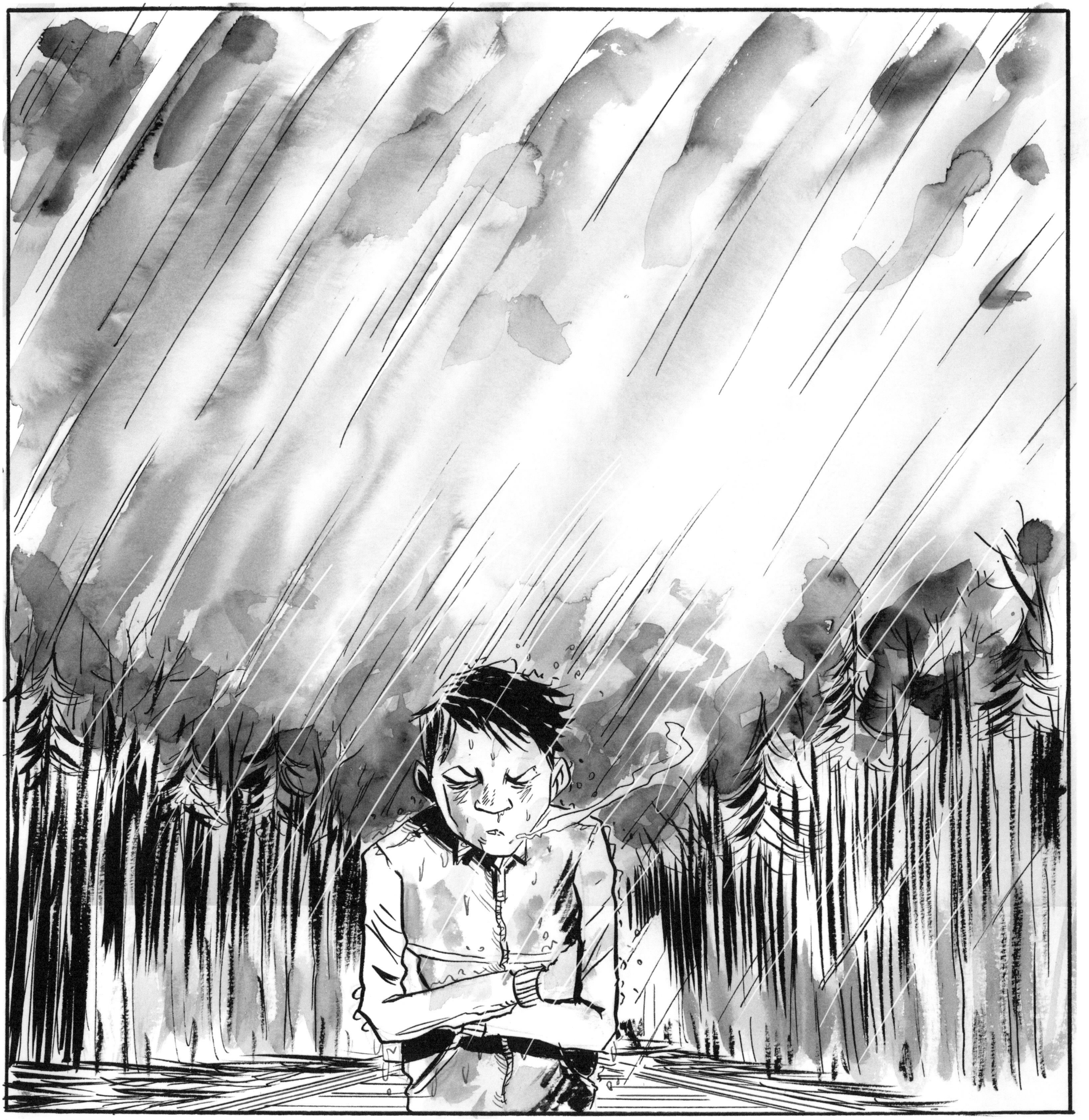

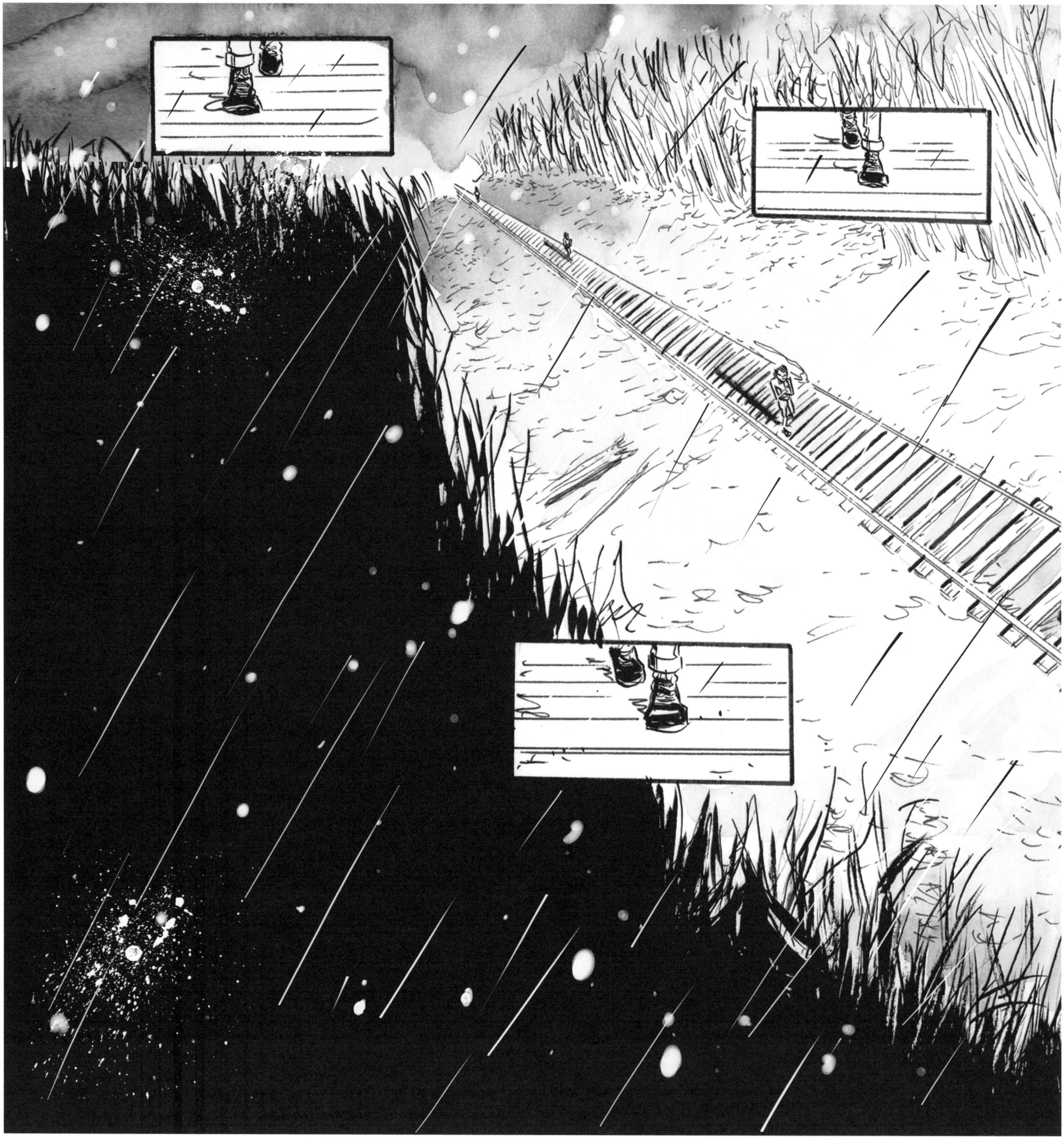

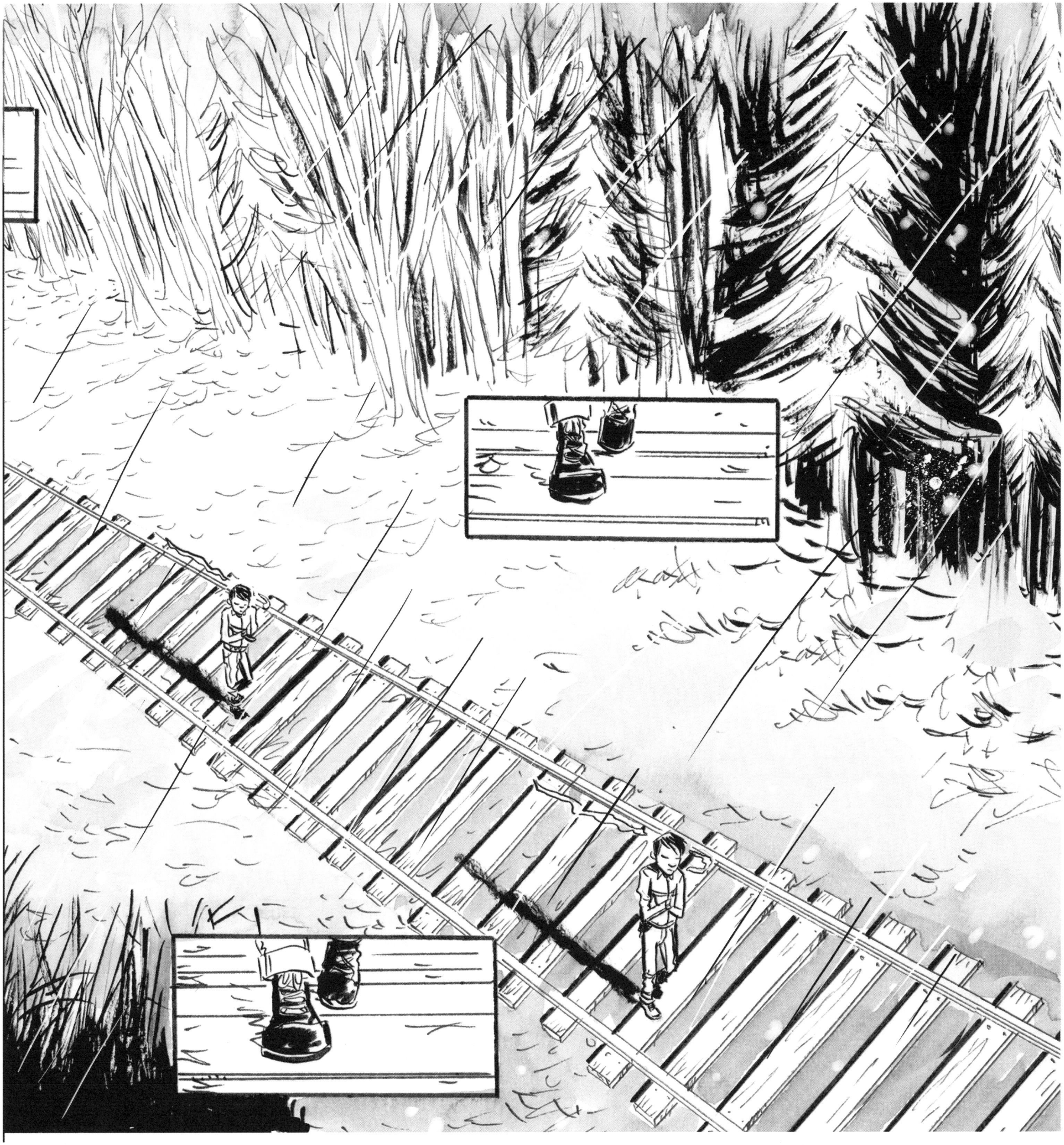

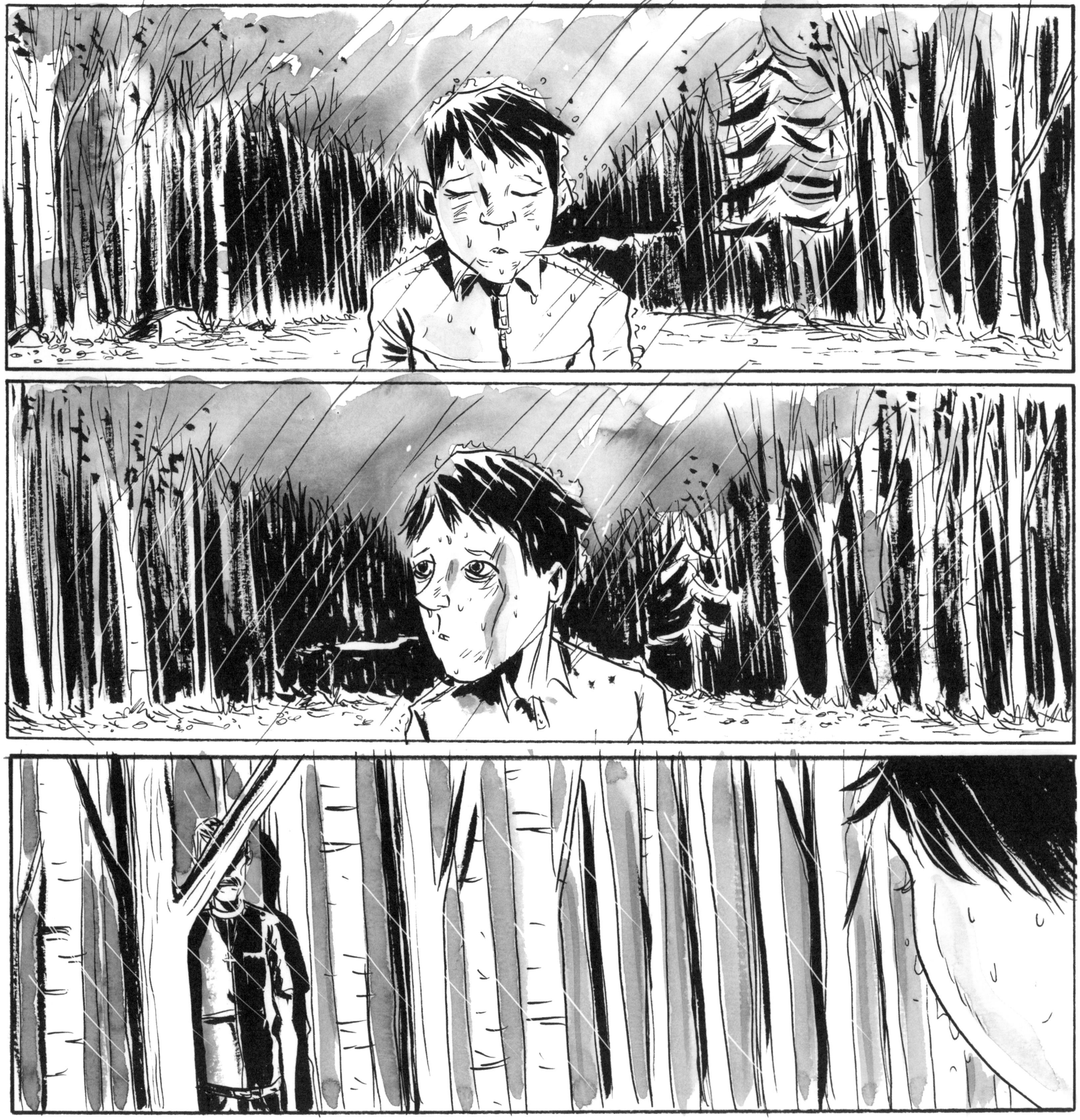

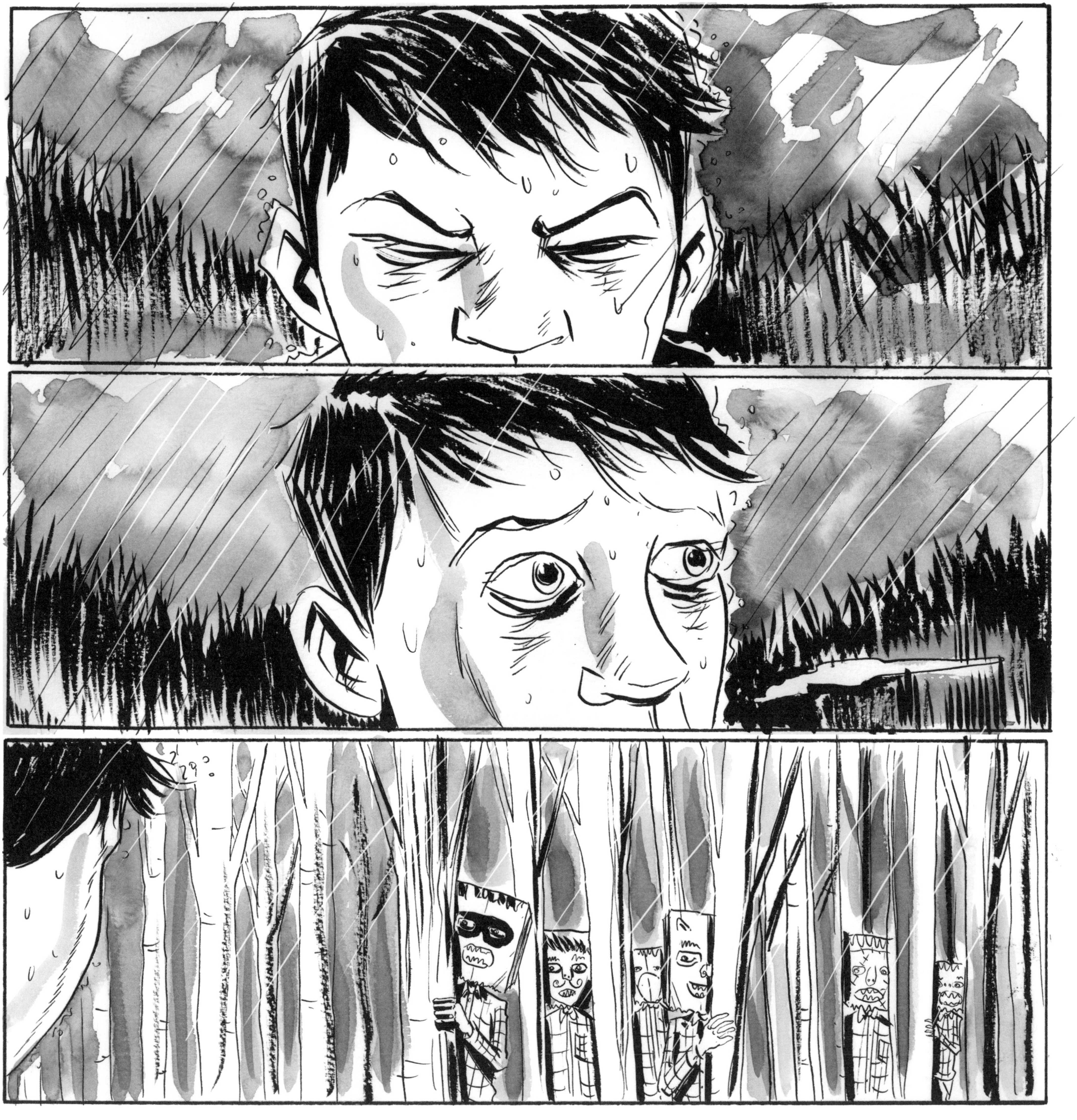

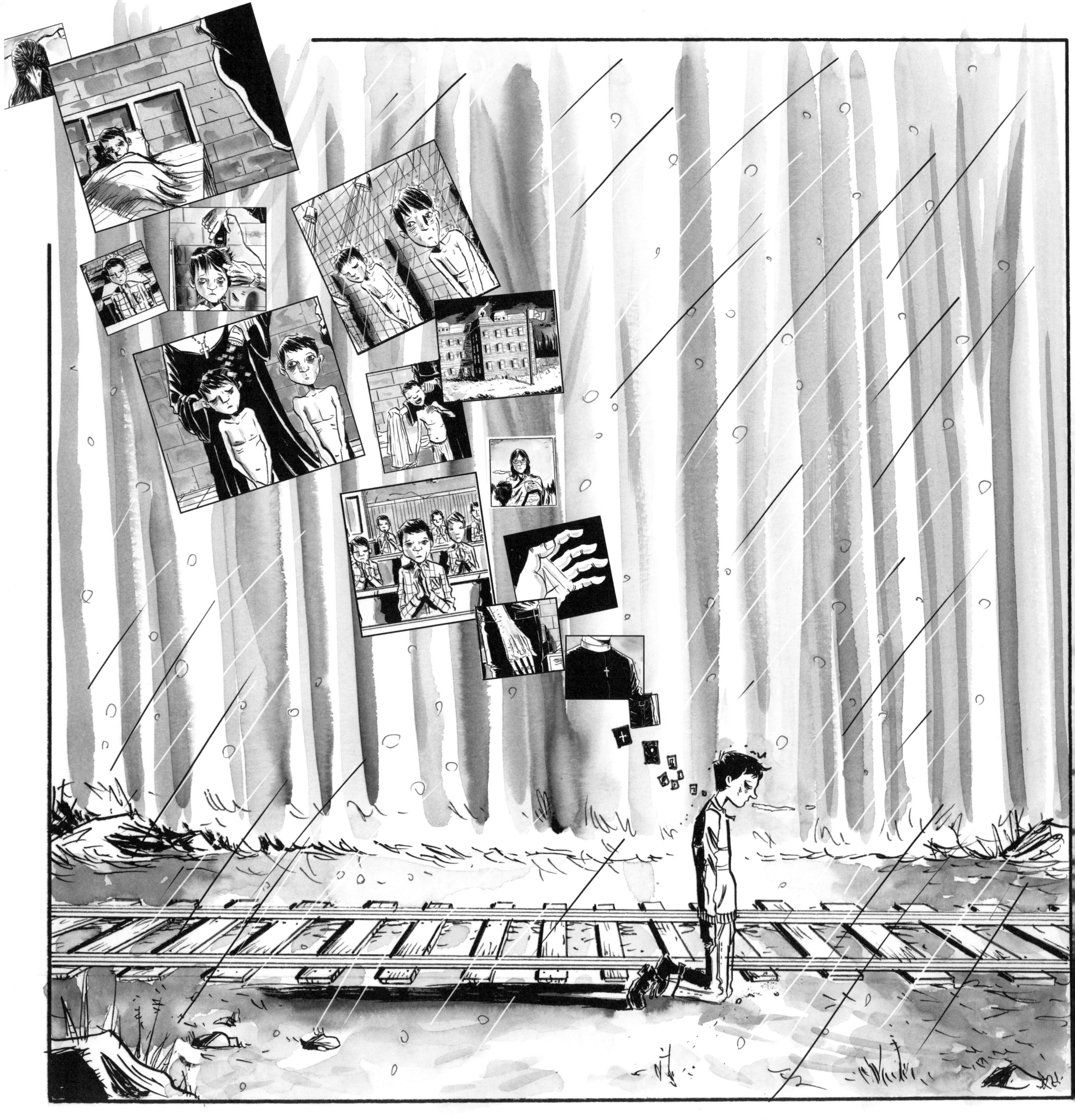

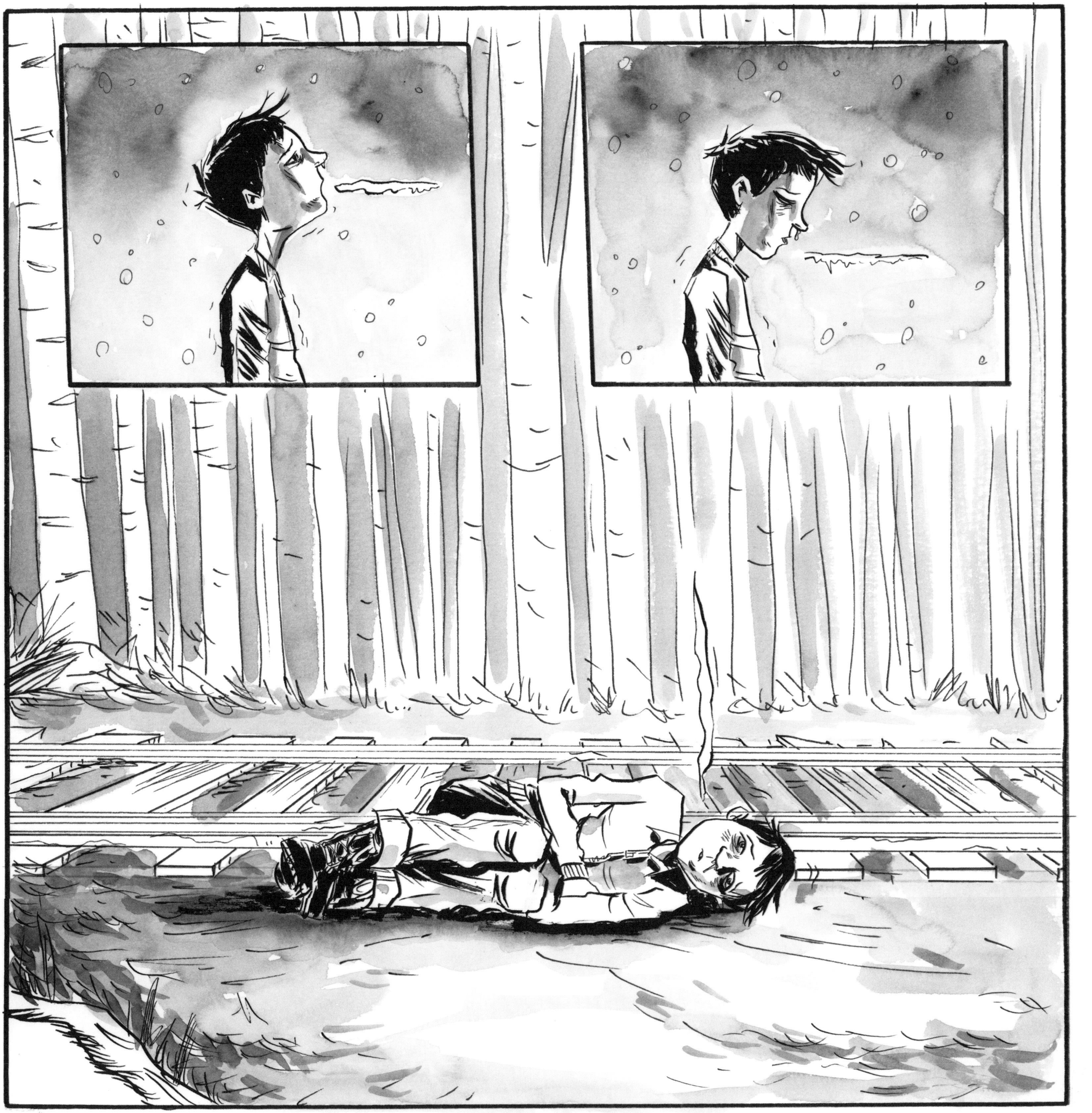

HERE, HERE AND HERE

I feel
Here, here and here

I hurt
Here, here and here

I lived
Here, here and here

I died
Here, here and here

You sign
Here, here and here

Here
Here, here and here

Here
Here, here and here

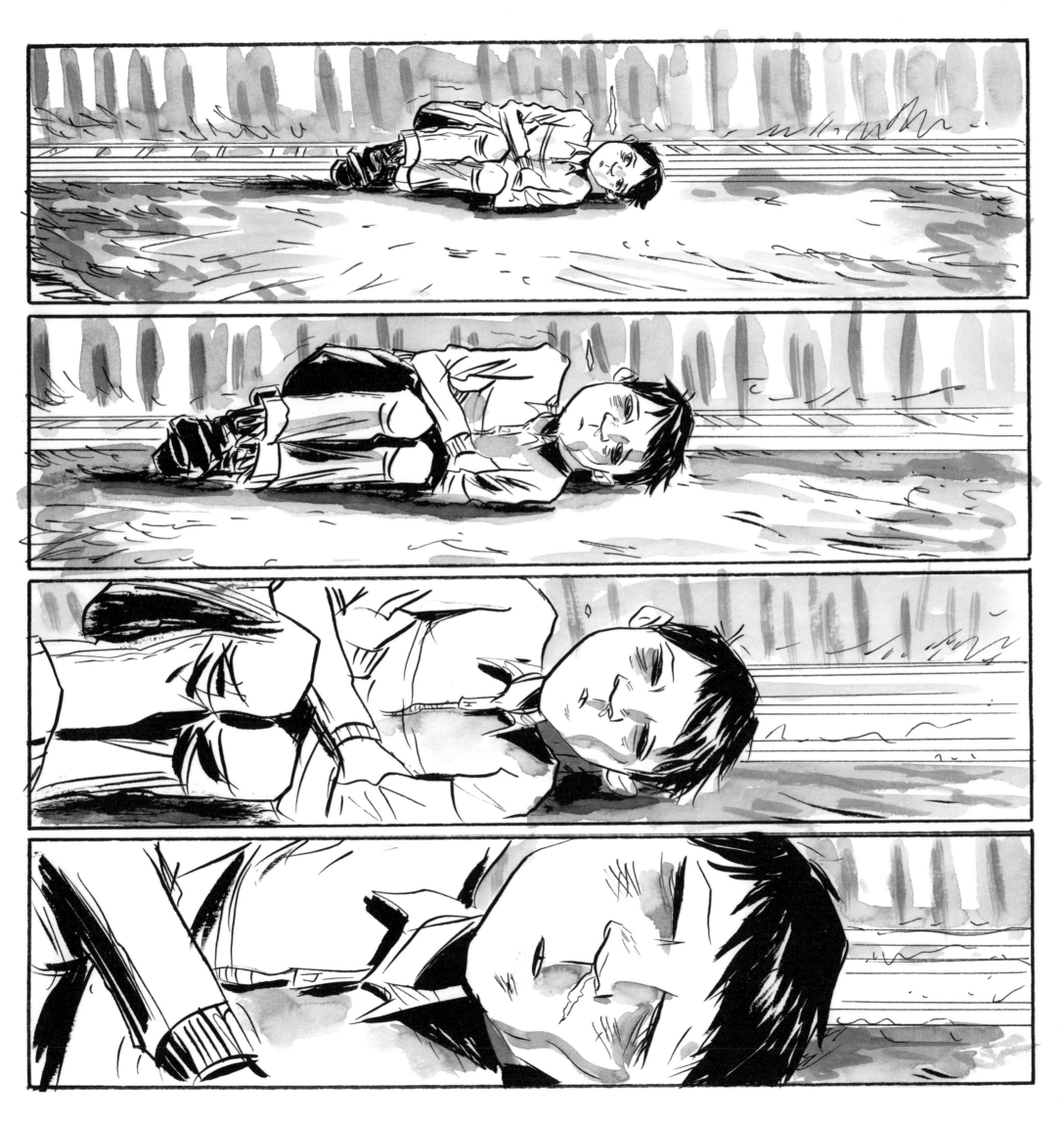

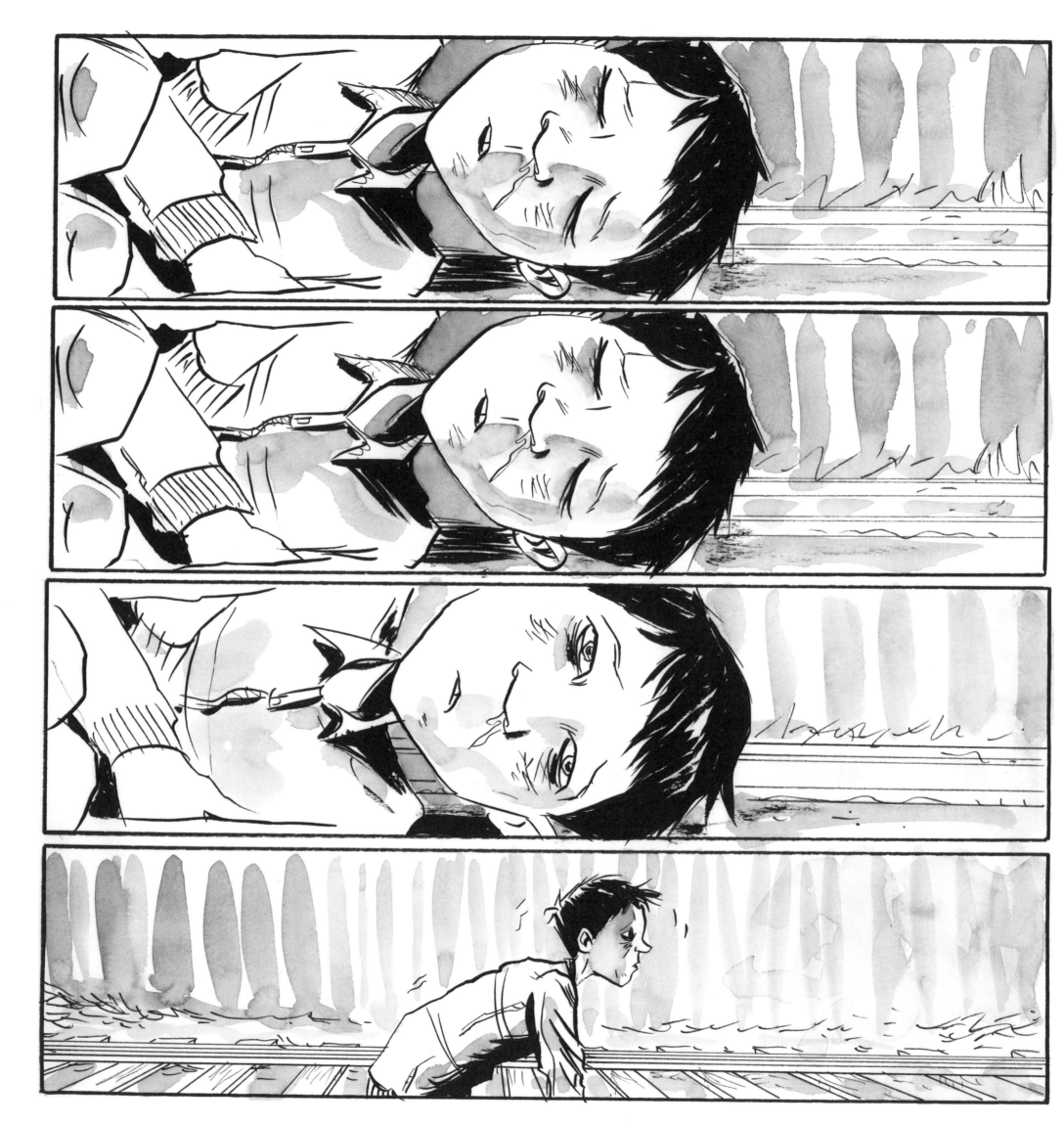

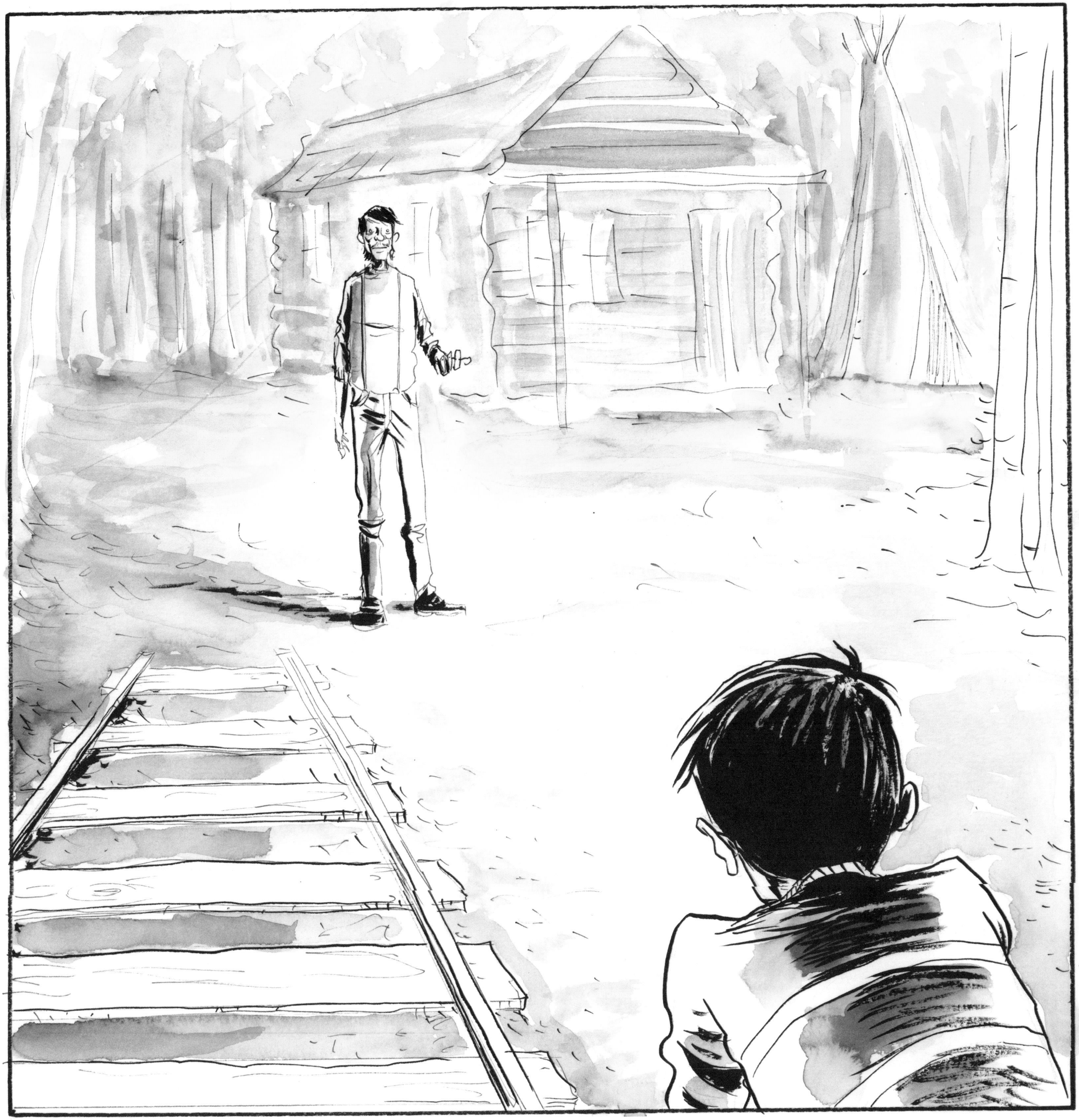

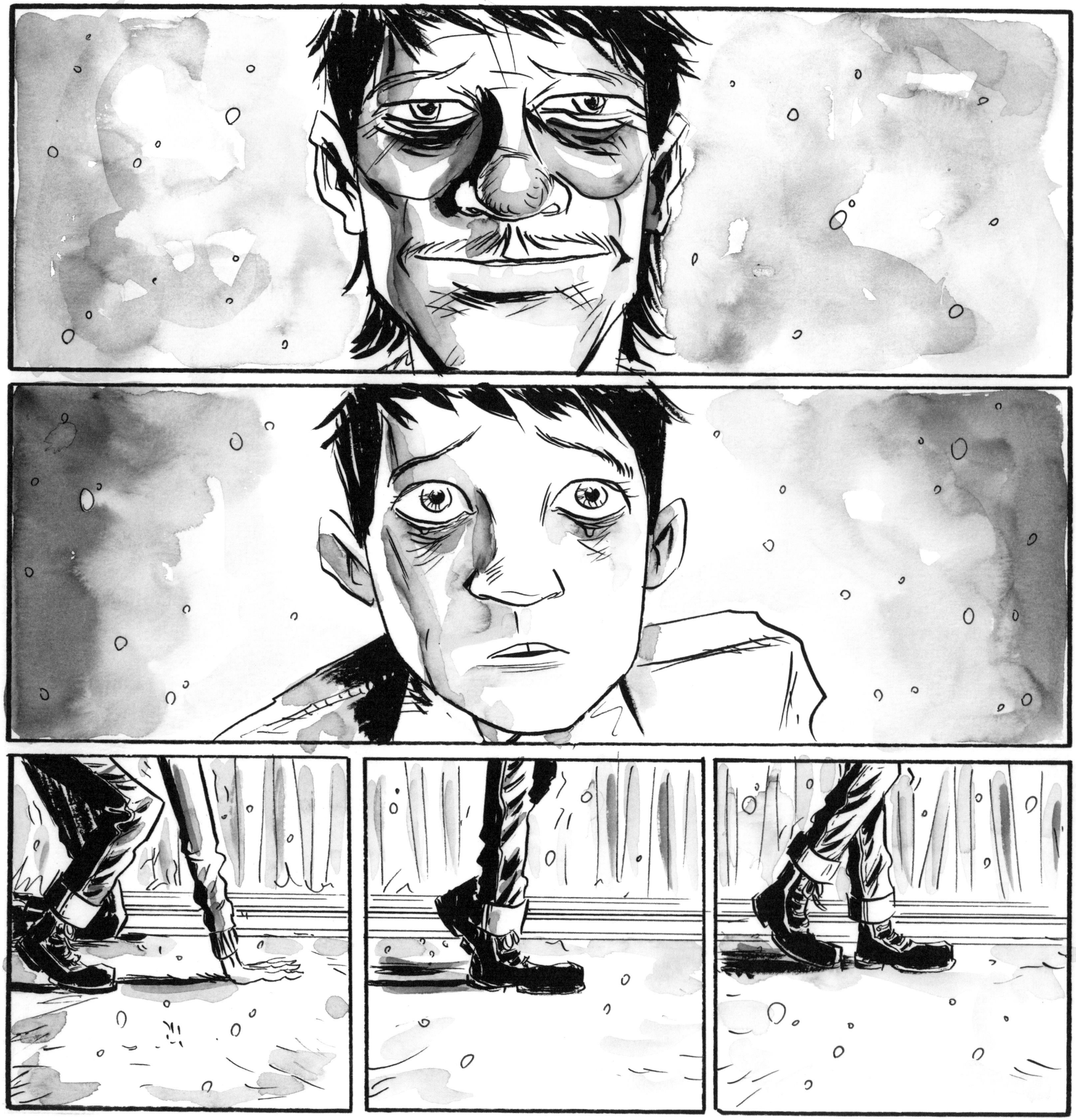

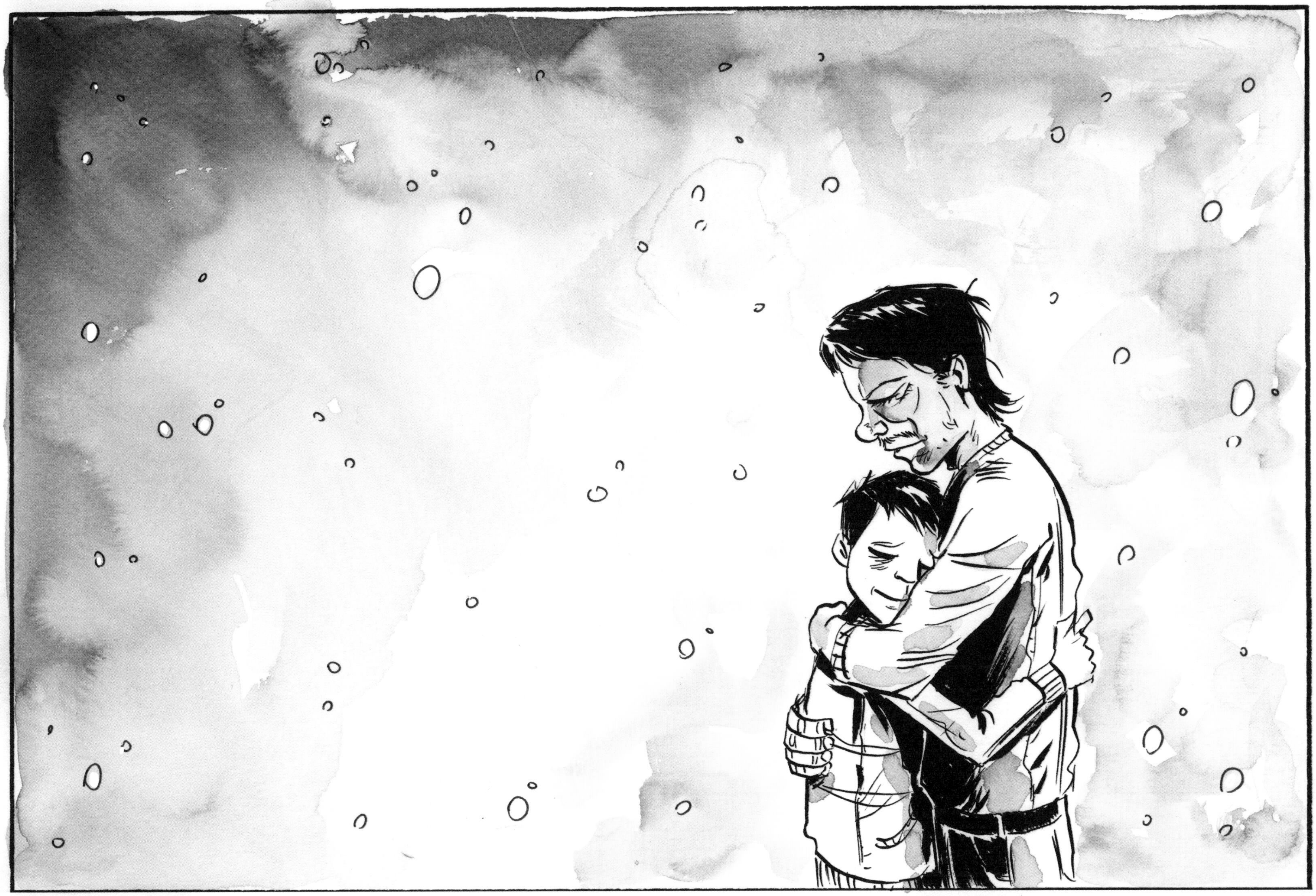
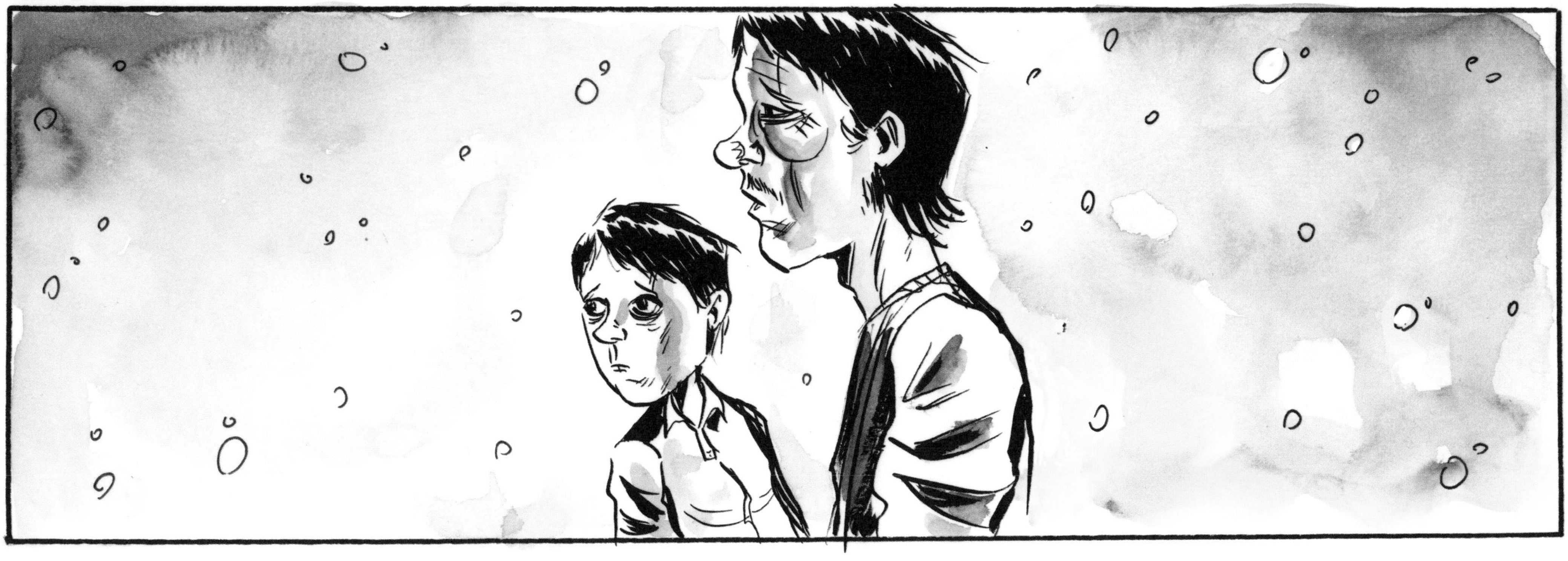

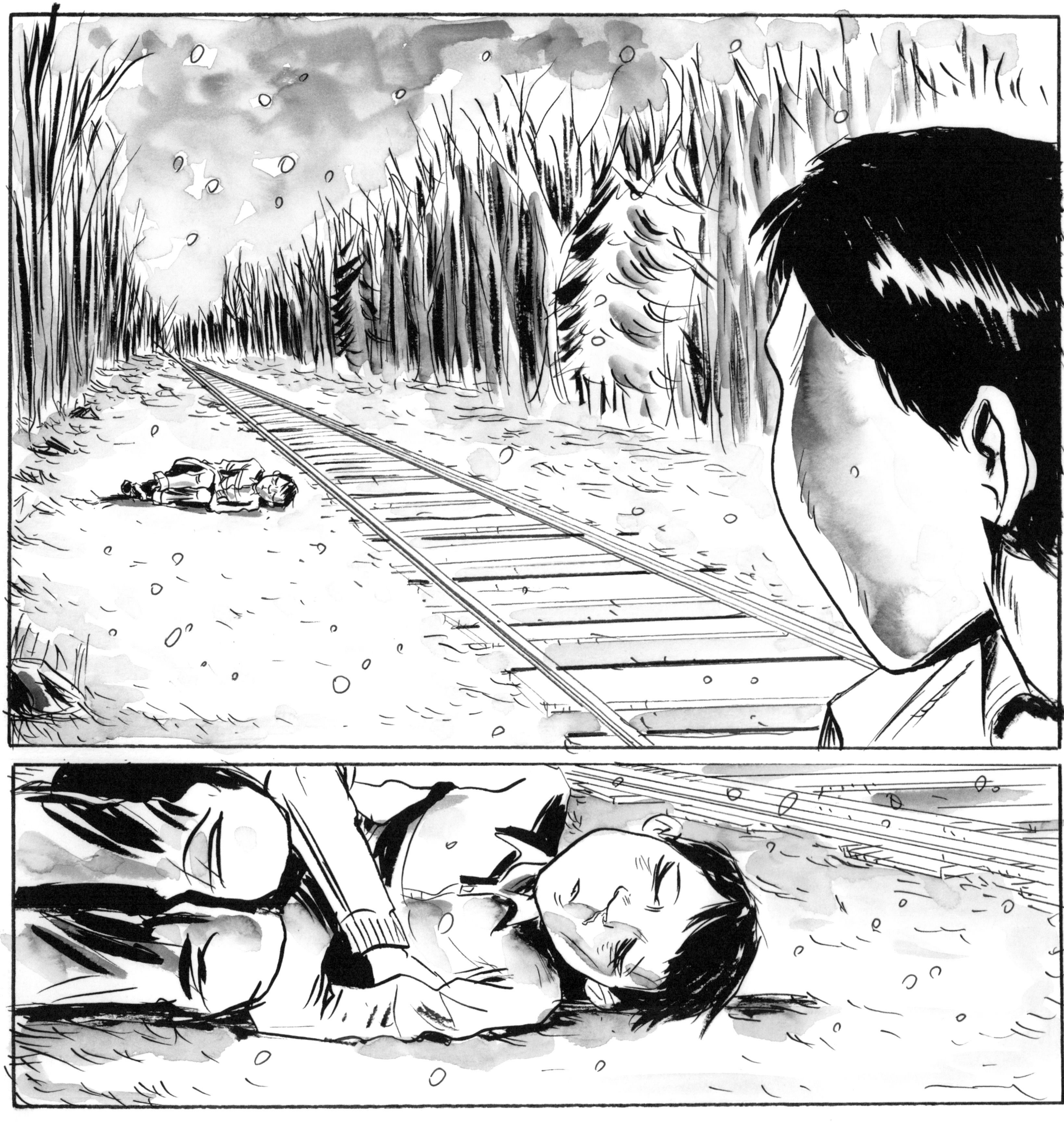

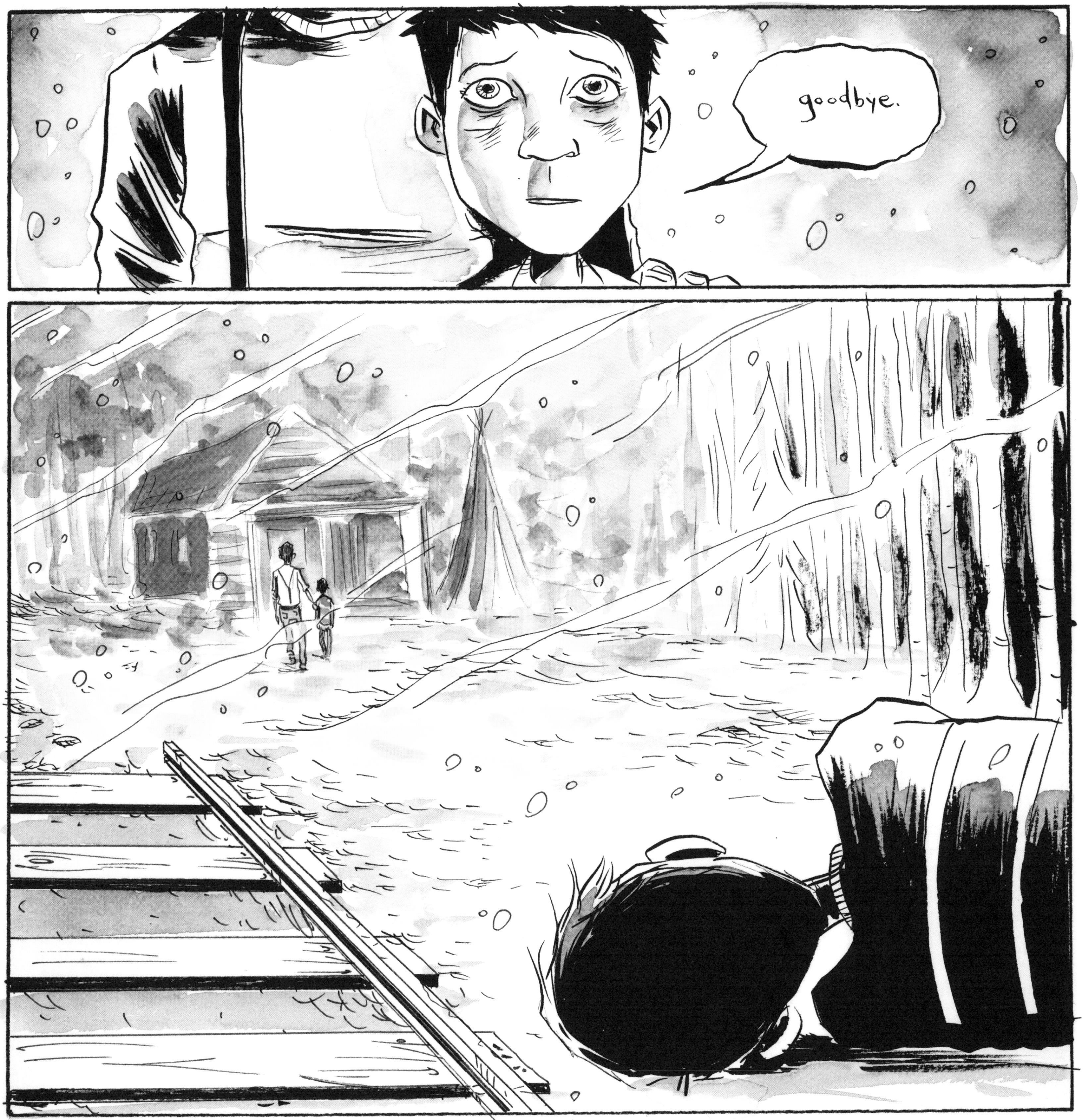
goodbye.

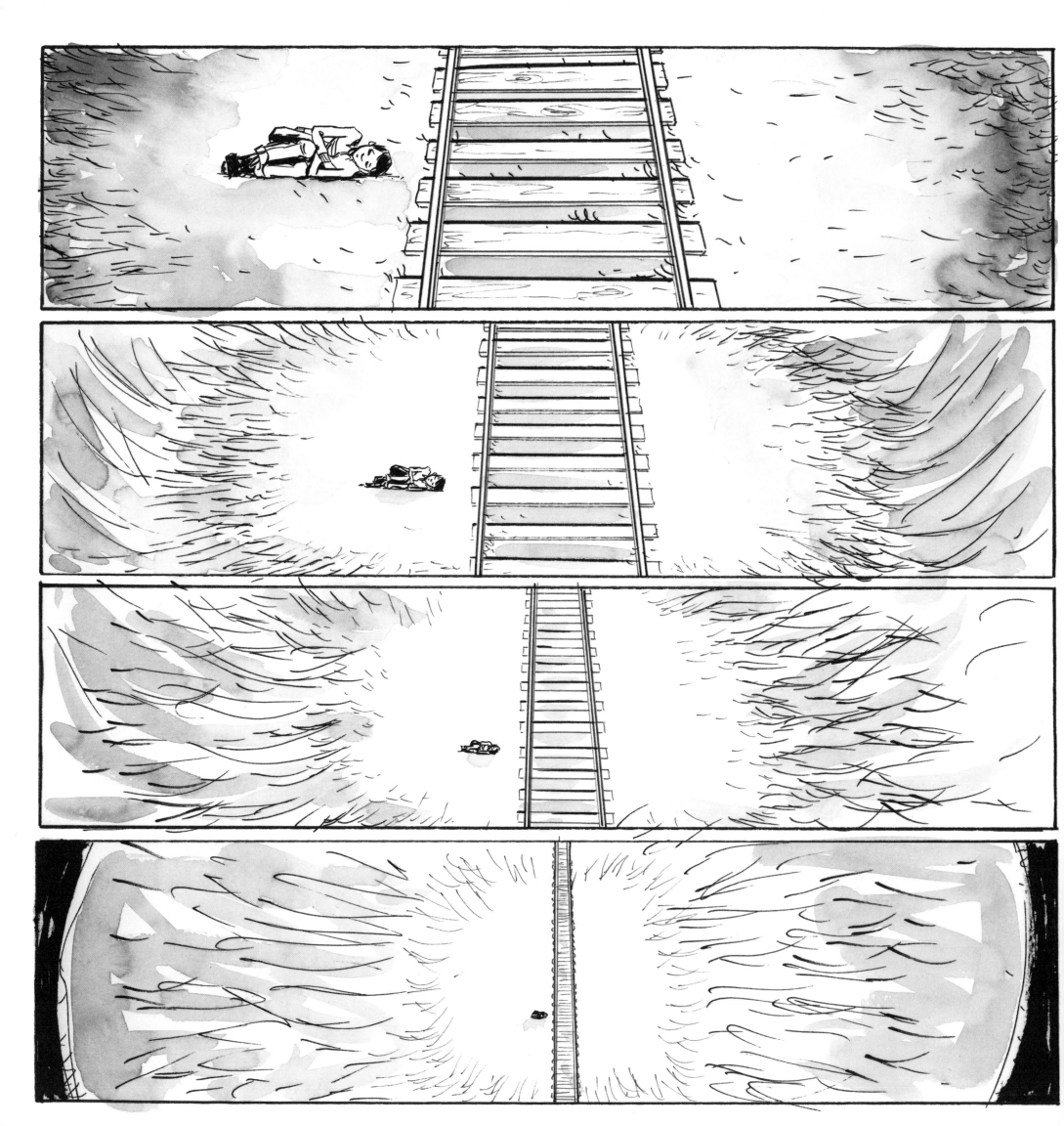

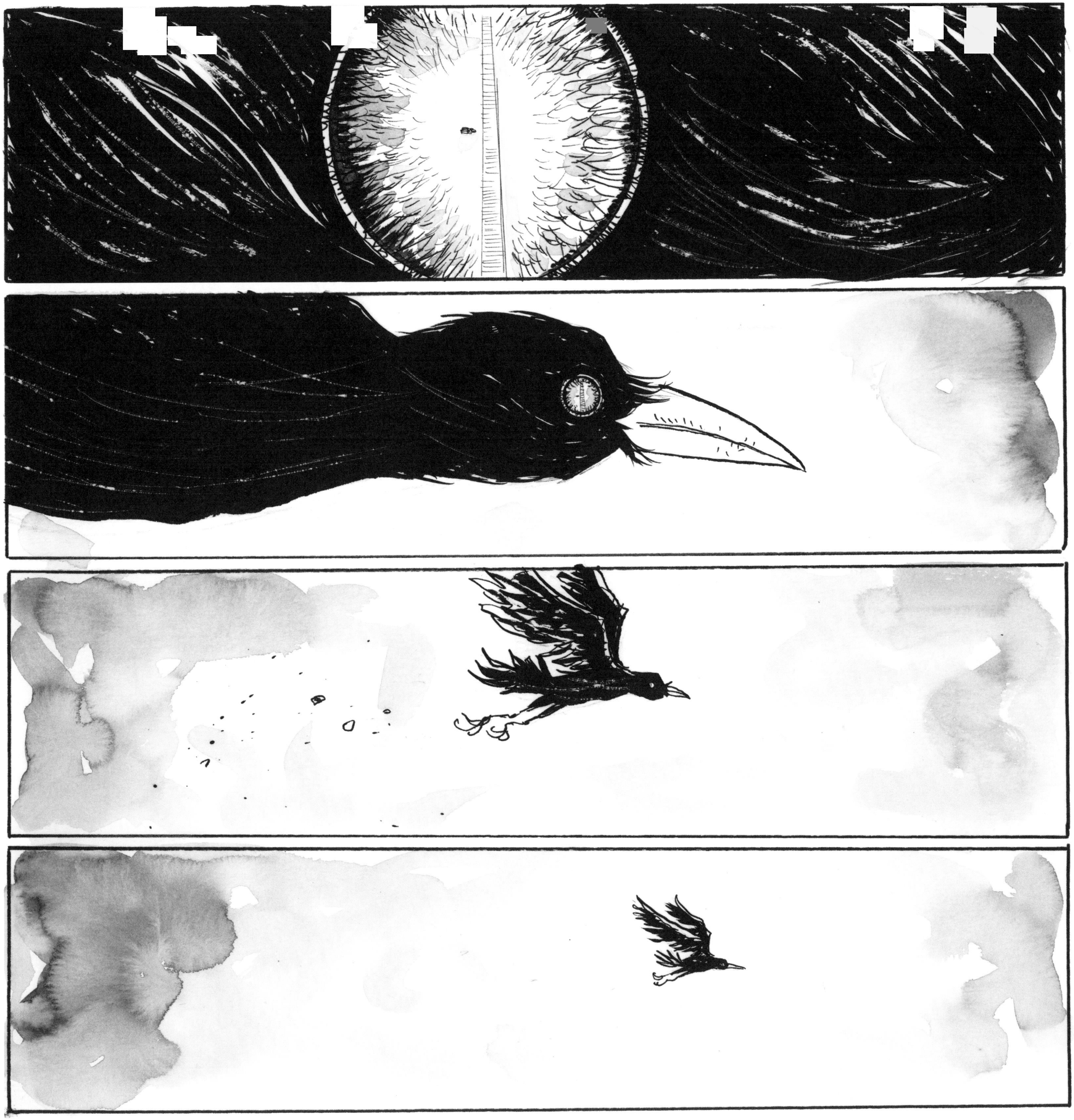

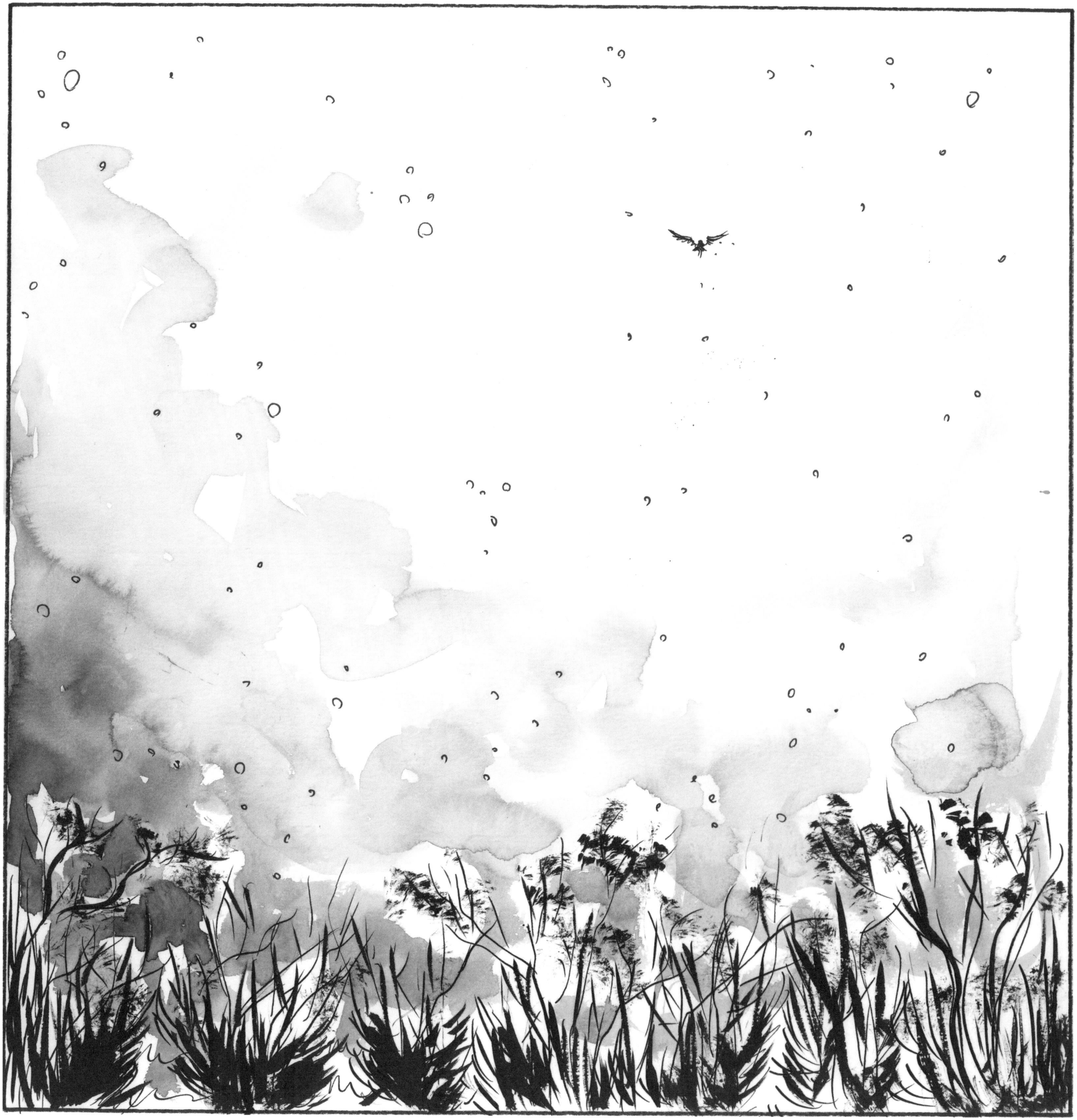